Chapter 1

From the outside, it looks rather grand, a repurposed hotel from an almost unimaginable era when people came here to holiday rather than merely for its proximity to the capital. The façade and entrance have been pleasantly reworked to ease the guilt of the many fretful adults who drop their loved ones here to see out their days in relative comfort. It is situated on the hinterland between city and countryside so that the residents can enjoy unspoilt views over the flatlands stretching out towards a distant coastline, whilst their families can easily access roads that take them far from this place. Convenience is the thing.

Underground, neatly arranged substrata mock the plight of the residents of St Peters. Once agile plesiosaurs have found themselves caught fast in ancient clay; mere inches above, axe heads and flints mark the early signs of a growing civilisation which has reached its zenith in a comfortably furnished retirement home in which the elderly can gracefully enjoy 24 hour care and a wide array of entertainments under the efficient supervision of trained and highly motivated staff without feeling beholden to their children, apart from the hefty monthly fees it requires to maintain them. So sayeth the glossy brochures and the friendly welcoming staff who maintain the Reception area.

By random good luck, one such fortunate person is being settled in right this minute, carefully wiping away a little tear as she is led by wheelchair through those very double doors. Her family wave cheerfully and then make haste to their oversized gas-guzzling vehicle to treat themselves to drive-thru coffee and donuts on their way home. The Americanised spelling is just one of the gifts the all-powerful franchisers have bestowed upon us; ubiquity is another. This is Anywhere. And it is Nowhere.

Behind the doors adjacent to the front desk, double doors lead to an arc of rooms arranged to accommodate eight living areas which in turn house four individual rooms, each identical apart from the personal belongings and trinkets which decorate them. In the centre stands a staff hub with one-way windows so that staff can go about their duties and keep an eye on the residents whilst maintaining a sense of professional privacy. Every morning, the residents are supported to make themselves ready for the day according to their individual needs and spend the day in the living area with their three friends or same-sex cohabitees. Most afternoons, they are offered various activities based on the whims of the staff in a larger area in the very centre of the establishment which can accommodate nearly a hundred people in an outdoor setting with pleasant gardens and comfortable wipe-down furniture.

At the rear of the complex, adjacent to the waste bins and the room which temporarily houses the residents who have outstayed their welcome and await merely the arrival of the black car to take them to their final accommodation, stands an annex. It has a separate entrance accessed from a service road. Officially, this is known as The Hereward Annex, more modest and consequently more affordable accommodation for residents who have taken less care to provide for their old age or whose families feel a little less obliged to them for more reasons than is polite to list. Unofficially, some of the residents refer to the place as Peterloo, not so much for any resemblance to the massacre which took place in the early 19th century up north but because they frequently have reason to complain of being treated like shit by the hardworking and efficient staff of St Peters. You won't find this place in the glossy brochures. Legally, it is held under separate ownership, although like St Peters it is operated by Caveo, along with several local schools, a shopping mall, and even the nearby prison.

The day is pleasantly warm and the residents of a jumble of rooms designated The Hereward Annex are sitting outside on tattered chairs staring out over a nondescript landscape under a huge sky littered with lenticular clouds.

'It should be inspiring,' says one of the residents in a weary tone. Despite the hour, he is wearing a silk dressing gown with an oriental design, purple with golden features. His face is likeable, still bearing the memory of the handsome arrangement of features of his distant past around the eyes and corners of his mouth. He has a thick thatch of hair, mostly turned to grey, and is clean shaven. Though the inevitable battle with gravity has begun in earnest, his body still retains some of the strength that must have made him quite a formidable specimen in his youth.

'Should be, Wormwood,' agrees one of his companions, 'but really isn't. It looks like someone has stretched a shroud over the landscape.' This is James Hunter. He has a kindly face, with laughter lines creasing his face. In the useful phase of his life, he was an electrician. Now he spends long days feeling the electrical impulses in his head misfiring as holes appear in his memory and things he once took for granted now require a force of will that can be exhausting.

The door opens to their left and a member of staff comes in to fuss over them. She is of indeterminate middle age at that point in life when time has sucked any natural grace or prettiness out of her. There is never enough time in her day to complete all her tasks, and she makes no secret of resenting the opposite in those for whom she is paid to care.

'Still in your dressing gown I see, Mr Wormwood,' she admonishes. A name tag identifies her as Amanda Richardson.

'It's a dressing gown kind of day.' Not bothering to look at her, he is casual in his tone, flippant. 'Why don't you fuss over George for a little while?' He gestures with his head towards the fourth room which contains a man lying in bed. He has been there for three years and they have never seen him up and about, never heard him speak.

'You know that's not his name,' says Amanda. 'He has a name. A perfectly good name. His name is Ken.'

'He's George to me,' says Wormwood.

She enters the man's room and closes the door behind her to give her some privacy and some respite from Wormwood's goading. They can hear her struggling to turn him.

An asian man next to Wormwood touches him on the arm. 'I've been meaning to ask you about that,' he says. 'Why do you call him George?' He is a relatively new arrival, replacing the likeable William Jones who had been notoriously terrible at poker and had metaphorically cashed in what few chips he had remaining in the cold snap at the start of the calendar year.

'I'm afraid the person formerly known as Ken is long dead,' says Wormwood coldly. 'He just doesn't know it.'

'Yes, but why George?'

'Listen to him,' says Wormwood. As Amanda goes about her business, turning him to avoid bed sores and providing at least the illusion that he is still alive, they can hear him groaning. 'That's the only sound he ever makes. Moaning, like some bloody zombie. The living dead.'

'Yes, but why George?'

Wormwood turns to look at him. 'You never watch any zombie films?' He raises an eyebrow.

'George Romero,' says James. 'Godfather of the zombie film. That's why. You'll find out soon enough. I think *'Day of the Dead'* has been lined up for this week.' He gestures with his head towards a stack of horror DVD's next to the TV, Wormwood's infamous Friday night film specials.

The asian man is nonplussed. 'What is it with you and names? You tried to call me Andy when I first arrived. Bloody cheek, if you ask me.' James helpfully tries to explain Wormwood's thesis that once admitted to Peterloo, there is a systematic attempt to dehumanise them. Only three personal items. Staff referring to them as Mr. Hunter and so on. 'Once they strip you of your name, you belong to them,' James explains. 'Without a name, you are no longer the person you used to be. You are whatever they want you to be. Weak. Needy. Compliant.'

'That's it, more or less,' says Wormwood. 'And to be fair, you have got an unpronounceable name.'

'No, I haven't. You're just lazy. I've seen those books you read, my friend. You are quite capable of remembering a simple name.' There is a fondness to the argument, two acquaintances playing out roles as a new friendship develops.

'Ashok?' says Wormwood. 'What kind of name is that?'

'It means: *He who is without sorrow.*'

'Yeah, well, that's ironic, seeing as you ended up in this dump. You'll know all about sorrow soon enough.' He goes on to expound on his view that the names they were given at birth are no longer valid as they sit here, waiting for the inevitable, their precious memories fading, even their sense of their own personalities evaporating like cheap aftershave. 'You think I'm really called Wormwood?'

'Yes, because you are,' says Ashok. 'I've seen it on official correspondence.' He puts on what he imagines to be an official voice: "Dear Mr Wormwood, we would like to remind you that being rude and disrespectful to staff is not tolerated at St Peters. Any further incidents of this nature will result in a loss of privileges."

They spend most days like this, finding new ways to kill time by creating pointless arguments and philosophical discussions rooted in an era when political correctness existed as tedious jokes about baldness. Part of Wormwood's antagonism towards Amanda stems from the fact that she reported him for racism after she witnessed a debate with Ashok about who would win a fistfight between Jesus and Ganesha.

'Even crucifixion didn't kill Jesus,' Wormwood had argued. 'He could easily beat someone as slow as an elephant.'

'Technically, I think it did kill him,' James disagreed.

'You just saw that in a film. He came back to life, remember?'

'You mean, like a zombie,' asks James.

'I hadn't thought of it like that, but now you mention it, yes', Wormwood jested, 'But a good zombie. A spiritual zombie, you might say.'

Her fingers on the cross she wore around her thickened neck, Amanda had shouted at them to stop. 'Don't be so disrespectful.'

Wormwood pretended to be crushed. 'But you, of all people, should be on my side.'

'Jesus was a man of peace!'

'Even if he was under attack from an elephant god trying to gore him with its tusks? I think not'

'*His* tusks,' Ashok corrected. He was a quick learner. He was going to fit in perfectly.

They also believe – with some justification - that Amanda can be unduly rough with those in her care, especially George, who clearly physically suffers under her supervision, hence the moaning. Other staff are generally given a much easier time, because they are nicer. Compared to most of the residents, Hereward is relatively easy to manage because their care needs are moderate.

Chapter 2

Probably due to some residual notion of the sabbath and duty and all that, Sunday is the main visiting day, although visits from loved ones are technically permitted at any time. They have relocated to the garden. Ashok is obscured behind a host of loved ones feeding him home-cooked delicacies which are generously shared with his new friends. As has become a sort of custom, James' daughter arrives late, flustered and apologetic, looking increasingly worn around the edges. He worries about her but tries not to show it. She has lost weight in the past few weeks and he tries to turn this into a compliment although she seems to recognise the concern in his tone and turns her eyes away.

'No kids?' he asks, disappointed.

'Football,' she explains. 'Their father wanted to treat them.' The choice of words is so impersonal that he can't help but notice. *Their father.* Not Barry.

He tries to make light of it. 'And here I was thinking that coming to see me was their treat.' She leans forward and fusses with his hair, what little remains, trying to train it to sit neatly across his scalp. There is great tenderness between them.

Wormwood sits alone. He has never received a visitor, although it is understood that he has been a family man in his younger days. It is not done to ask him about what has transpired to create this isolation. If he chooses to discuss personal matters, that is another thing. But he never does. He chooses to sit outside regardless, taking in the sun. To his left, about twenty feet away, he sees a boy sitting alone, looking bored close to despair. It is a sensation he knows only too well.

'I've got a question,' Ashok announces. 'It's an important one. I think Amanda raised a valid question Why *do* we have to be so puerile all the time?'

James answers for Wormwood as if it has all been pre-rehearsed. 'Because every time you laugh, somewhere in the world a petty bureaucrat dies.'

Ashok laughs. 'Of course,' he says, as if the answer was self-evident.

'And there's no easier way to raise a laugh than a bit of stupid puerile humour,' says Wormwood. 'That's just how it is.' To punctuate his point, he raises a buttock and farts, and the whole room erupts.

okay as long as they play along in the weekly bingo and craft sessions that are quite literally ways of killing time. Ashok has proven himself already to be a more than capable enabler of Wormwood's worst instincts, frequently joining him in his ongoing attempts to alleviate the crushing weight of time by gently provoking others. He understands that it is a game that his friend is playing.

She stops on her way out and confronts him. 'Any more of this and I will report you to Mr Lord.'

'Again, you mean?'

'Yes. Again. You knew very well that you are no longer permitted to socialise with Mr Beckford and that the consumption of vodka is absolutely prohibited.'

'Very good,' says Wormwood flippantly. 'Excellent pun.' He encourages the others in the room to join him in a round applause for her inadvertent wordplay. 'It was Absolut Vodka we were drinking, as it happens. Windrush is quite the connoisseur and will drink nothing else.' He really knows how to push her buttons, which he would argue is her fault for being such a predictable and sanctimonious little robot. Defiantly, she stands over him. He thinks briefly about rising to his feet. 'You have already been warned.'

'Leave her be, Wormwood.' James plays a different role, the mediator, but afterwards he joins in the laughter.

'Loss of privileges? Big deal. We spend all day shut up in here like inmates in a bloody prison. What exactly do you think you could take away from me that I haven't already lost?'

The door is shut quite forcefully behind her.

'One of these days...' James chuckles.

Wormwood clutches his chest in mock pain. 'I should be so lucky.'

The door opens and Amanda remerges, looking slightly flushed.

'And what have you two been up to in there?' asks Wormwood with a knowing wink. 'Judging by the noises the two of you were making...' He lets his voice trail into innuendo.

'Why do you have to be so puerile all the time?' she snaps at him.

'Ha. Puerile? Me? That's ironic, don't you think. Is this more puerile that expecting us to be content playing bingo and sit-down keep-fit and doing bloody jigsaw puzzles. We're old, we're not morons.' She despises what she wrongly perceives as his self-pity. The room is in hearing distance of the dementia room, where the residents can do little more than groan and shout incoherently all day long. Things can always be worse. 'Why don't you just grow up or shut up!' she snaps.

'We've done all the growing we're ever going to do.' Wormwood makes no attempt to conceal his contempt for her in his tone of voice, unable to accept that she genuinely can't see the difference between feeling sorry for himself and his resentment at being infantilised. 'It's all downhill from here.'

'You know what I mean,' she retorts.

'And so do you, Nurse Richardson. You could try going easy on him, poor old bastard.' He has a way of pronouncing her name under his breath, in a way which obscures the fact that he frequently refers to her as Nurse Ratshit. It does not go unnoticed. Very little does. Wormwood's role is mischief-maker. They all have one foot in the grave, he cheerfully reminds them, so they should take their laughs while they can, however they can. Death, that most unwelcome of guests, has become such a regular visitor that he says they have to embrace it, in their horror film nights, in their vodka nights, in the endless banter, in their dreams. He simply isn't prepared to play along with the infantilising attitude of St Peters and the moronic pretence that everything will be

'Aren't you a bit young to be in here?' he asks. The boy is startled. He looks behind him and then understands that he is being addressed.

'Visiting,' he explains. He nods with his head towards a family group on the other side of the garden in that laconic way that only teenagers can do, as if it takes all the energy he can spare.

'Figured as much. Not feeling it?'

'Nah.' He shuts his eyes as if he is in physical pain. The embarrassment of being spoken to by some doddery old pensioner.

'Got any weed?' The old man shocks him out of his slumber.

'What?'

'Weed. You know.' He mimes smoking a spliff and letting his eyes go blank.

The boy sizes him up and shakes his head. 'Nah,' he says. 'Sorry.'

'Shame,' says Wormwood. 'Not for me, you understand. For my good friend over there.' Wormwood gestures towards the far corner of the garden where a greying rasta sits with the extended Beckford family. 'That's Windrush. A good friend of mine. Ex-roommate until they split us up for being bad influences on each other. They used to sort him out with his weed but they get searched when they come to see him now. Can you believe that?'

'Actually, I can,' says the boy. He is still trying to work out whether the old man is winding him up or for real. 'I can't tell if you're joking or not.'

'Neither can I sometimes.' Wormwood smiles. The boys pulls up his chair and comes to sit closer.

'You here to see your grandad?'

'Yeah. My mum made me come. I love him and all that, but it's just a bit boring.' He looks embarrassed by what he has just said. 'I didn't mean...'

Wormwood silences him with a hand. 'Don't apologise, he says. 'You're young, you should be out having fun somewhere.' Wormwood doesn't understand why he is making the effort; neither of them do. Perhaps the boy reminds him of someone he used to know. Simultaneously, he both envies and pities him his youth.

The boys shrugs his shoulders. 'Yeah.'

'He's only just got here and we haven't really talked but he does seem a bit dull. No offence.'

'None taken,' says the boy.

'Remember this, though,' Wormwood cautions him. 'He was probably just like you once. I bet he never once thought he would end up like this. A burden. An obligation. It's life that makes you boring.'

'I can see why you don't get many visitors,' says the boy.

'Look around,' says Wormwood. 'There's not much to do round here. Fun is in very short supply.' He nods again towards Windrush guffawing now with his family. 'He's a real character. A great laugh. But we upset some staff and now they say that if we so much as speak to each other they will stop his visits.'

'That can't be true,' says the boy.

'Sadly, that's the way things are.' Wormwood sits back in his chair, trying to find a way to get comfortable.

The boy looks at him. He has a pretty face that Wormwood knows will one day sag into blandness. He hopes he makes the most of it while he can. His eyes are blue with dark striations that glister. 'I'm really sorry,' he says.

'Yeah,' says Wormwood. 'Me, too. That's why I have to sit alone.' He nods in the direction of Windrush and pulls a clownish sad face. The boy gives a silent laugh.

A woman's voice calls out across the garden, annoyed. 'Jacob. Leave the man alone. Come and speak to your grandad.'

'It's fine,' Wormwood calls out to her. 'It's the other way round.' He can tell by the woman's face that it is not fine. 'It's me that's bothering him,' he explains.

'Nice to talk to you.' The boy stands up. He sticks out a hand awkwardly, obviously not used to any kind of formal greeting. 'It's Jake.'

'Likewise.' Wormwood takes his hand and squeezes hard. In a whisper, he adds, 'And next time, don't forget the bloody weed.'

The boy laughs out loud, his face transformed momentarily as he drags his chair across the grass and re-joins the fringes of his family group. Occasionally, he glances over and they share a conspiratorial smirk. Ashok's daughter comes over and offers Wormwood a delicacy. It is the best thing he has tasted in a very long time. He thanks her profusely and takes his time savouring every mouthful. There are flavours that interact with his mouth in ways that surprise him, reacquainting him with the idea that food can be something more than sustenance. A pleasure. He lets himself relax into the sun and allows the warmth to wash over him and, for the first time since whenever, he sleeps without dreaming.

Monday is a drag. The notion that this is the start of a new week torments them. Deprived of the structure of the working week, most days are indistinct from one another. For some of the residents, the pleasure of a family visit the previous day dissolves into the realisation that they have become a weekly chore - not a burden perhaps, but certainly an obligation. This is not to accept that there is no pleasure in these visits for that would be untrue, but all the same it is a familial inconvenience which has to be squeezed into an already stretched sequence of commitments.

Where does the time go?

There are some benefits to the imposition of some kind of routine, however. Today is Tuesday. Mid-morning. It is nearly time for her to come. No, not her. *She.* Like the character played by Ursula Andress in the film. The perfect woman.

They have never heard her speak and wonder if she is mute or merely unable to communicate in English. She is the deep-clean lady, divine wielder of the steam mop. Like some kind of higher being, she appears once a week with modern cleaning gadgets and gives the room a much-needed antiseptic wash-down. Though she never speaks and occasionally wears headphones - whether to protect her ears or to listen to pop music they neither know nor care - she always smiles at them as they facilitate her work by keeping out of her way and obligingly moving whatever objects they can manage in their diminished state.

There is nothing sexual in their admiration for her; such things are mercifully in their past. In truth, she is not exquisitely beautiful, but then women who know they are good-looking are rarely attractive. In her case, the whole is somehow more than the sum of her parts. With as much elegance and grace as can be mustered in work overalls and functional shoes, she carries out her work efficiently and well, and then is gone.

'Almost,' says Wormwood, when she is gone. 'I hate to objectify her or cheapen her with smutty obsession, but she is almost enough to light the spark, if you know what I mean.' In the gleam of chrome and the sparkle of floor tile, it is as if she has left some essence of herself in the room.

'I thought we agreed not to become dirty old men,' says James to the room. The voice of reason.

'Agreed,' says Wormwood. 'But we all used to be men once, you know.' The room falls silent.

When lunch arrives, it is usual meagre affair, made worse by new regulations concerning healthy eating which renders the food anodyne. Even James cannot muster any optimism.

'I thought I was losing my sense of taste,' he complains, 'But then your delightful family bring in food that actually has some flavour and I feel alive again.' Ashok smiles at the compliment. The lady passing round the trays tuts at their lack of gratitude, then when back at the central staff hub she will eat her own lunch which she has meticulously prepared for herself at home.

'Have you tried eating this stuff?' says Wormwood. 'We're not brats. We would just like something worth the effort of eating once in a while. We've seen the brochures. We know how the other half eat *over there*.' He gestures grumpily towards the part of the complex where the residents of St Peters enjoy a far higher standard of culinary fayre. The lady ignores him and leaves them to it.

At it happens, they know full well how the other half eat because Wormwood habitually goes off on raiding missions into St Peters and helps himself to whatever spare food is lying around, always making sure that his comrades are well fed, too. He has a system. He has learned the habits of residents in St Peters in terms of regular visits and knows when certain people will be taken out to lunch by loved ones, leaving behind perfectly edible food of far superior quality than they are used to in the Annex. Learning the code to access the main block from Peterloo was a piece of cake. The code changes weekly, but one particularly forgetful member of staff has taken to writing the code on a scrap of paper which she takes with her on her morning rounds. As long as he is careful to always return plates and cutlery – china and metal, no less – no one is any the wiser and Wormwood can enjoy the day knowing he has got one over on the bastards that run the place.

The afternoon is given over to philosophical discussion, of a sort. These are usually led by James and quickly taken over by Wormwood. Today's is on the subject of the possibility of an afterlife. James has never had a Hindu friend and is always delighted by the wisdom which Ashok can provide.

'You know that we believe in reincarnation, right?' Privately, he is astonished at his friend's ignorance. 'You know about samsara?'

James looks at him askance. 'I know you don't mean the perfume. I bought some once for my wife. Lovely.'

'Not the perfume, no. Samsara as in the infinite cycle of death and rebirth. For me, the idea of an afterlife is not something that I hope may be the case; it is an absolute certainty. If I have lived a good life, I will be reborn in a different body.'

'And did you?'

'Did I what?' asks Ashoke 'Live a good life? I believe so, yes. So, for me, I can sit here day after day knowing that as long as I continue to be a good man that I will be reborn when I die.'

James is impressed. 'That's nice,' he says. 'That must be really nice.' He is momentarily lost in contemplation of how very nice that must be for Ashok.

'Honestly, I don't know how you can bear the not-knowing,' says Ashok. He almost articulates what an agony it must be to believe in nothing, to have no sense of a greater design in which goodness is rewarded, but he thinks better of it.

James likes these discussions because his brain has been deprived of stimulus for much of his life and it gives him a sense that he somehow still matters as long as he keeps striving to develop a greater understanding of the world.

'I hope there's something after all this,' he says, gesturing around the room with its corporate blandness and the TV tuned to BBC news with subtitles on for the hard of hearing, or else daytime TV for the hard of thinking. 'I mean, I think I've lived a good life,' he says doubtfully, 'but who's to judge?'

'I can't pretend to know everything about you,' says Wormwood, 'but I'm pretty confident you haven't got any dead bodies buried under the patio. I suspect you have lived a pretty good life.'

'Good enough?'

'Why not.'

James brightens. 'So you think I'm off to heaven when all this is over?'

'God, no,' says Wormwood. 'When you're gone, you're gone. That's it.'

Ashok can't accept that. 'No,' he says. 'There has to be more to life than that. You are an intelligent man. You have a good soul. Your energy, your essence, cannot simply disappear. It changes. That's how it works.'

'For your sake, I hope that's true,' says Wormwood, 'But I can't believe in that. When we go, it's six feet under and that's the end of it.'

Ashok laughs, secure in his faith that he will shortly be back on earth. 'In your case, my friend,' he says, 'I think you may be going a lot further down than that.'

James is alarmed. 'Hell, you mean?'

'Well,' says Ashok, regarding the three stolen pates of food that Wormwood has appropriated for them, 'Theft is a sin.'

'But we ate the food,' says James with dismay.

'Ah yes, but it would have been a greater sin to waste food that a friend had offered to you.'

James falls silent, thinking. 'I can't tell if you're joking or not.'

'Neither can I, sometimes.' Ashok nudges Wormwood who sits just within reach. 'That's your bad influence.'

'What does it mean, to live a good life?' asks James. 'I mean, I never broke the law. I never beat my wife. I tried to be good. I worked hard. Is that enough?'

Wormwood sighs. 'Let's see. Did you ever covet your neighbour's oxen?'

'My neighbour never had oxen. She had a cat, though.'

'Alright. Did you ever covet her pussy?'

'Are you being rude, Wormwood?'

'Of course not. I'm just being biblical.' He changes tack. 'Did you give to charity?'

'Well, I bought a Big Issue once.'

'And did you enjoy it?'

'You know, I really did. It was quite interesting.'

'Okay, that's covered then,' says Wormwood. 'I think you are fine.'

James reaches down and picks up his copy of the Daily Mail. 'It's just that I read this sometimes and I wonder if everything I thought was right turns out to have been wrong. I mean, it says that we've basically destroyed the planet. I look at my grandkids and think: did I kill the planet for them before they were old enough to enjoy it?'

It's a sobering thought. 'Well, I guess we'll find out soon enough,' says Wormwood. He rises a little awkwardly to his feet and starts collecting the plates. 'I'd better get these back before they're missed.' He walks with a slight but noticeable limp towards the door.

'If the earth does die, Ashok, will it be reborn,' he asks, 'as long as it's been good?'

Ashok smiles. 'You know, that's a pretty good question. I may have to consult the holy scriptures on that one.' Though he is in good spirits, he doesn't look so well this evening. Even his banter is punctuated by an alarming cough.

'Bloody lungs,' he says weakly. 'Bloody inhospitable climate.'

'You're cold?' says James with incredulity. 'It's sweltering this evening.' He is right. The room is uncomfortably warm and there is no sign of a breeze to ease the discomfort.

'Sweltering?' repeats Ashok in a frail voice. 'Believe me, this is not hot. It's all relative, my friend.' In St Peters, the rooms are climate controlled to ameliorate the cold in Winter and the heat in the Summer, or whatever passes for those seasons in this new dystopian world where ancient rhythms have been thrown out of balance. In Peterloo, one way or another they suffer all year round.

Wormwood wanders off in search of a drink. When he has left the room, James asks if Ashok really believes that Wormwood is hell-bound.

'If you don't believe in heaven,' he says kindly, 'then there can be no fear that you will end up in Hell. Don't worry.'

But he's mistaken. Wormwood does believe in Hell. He's thinks he's already there.

Chapter 3

There are good days and bad days, relatively speaking. For Wormwood, there are whole weeks when his mind is as keen as it ever was - sharp enough to eviscerate fools - although even that is a mixed blessing because there are always things in our pasts best forgotten. As is his way, he fights to maintain a sense of the man he used to be, and that perhaps is the problem. Others have family to remind them of the various roles they played in former times - husband, workmate, father, whatever. But Wormwood, living in splendid isolation, has to be self-reliant. It bothers him. It feels like a coiled serpent in his mind; when it twists or slithers, there are voids. Increasingly, he has to make a specific effort to recall significant people or events that leave him literally gasping at the cruelties of time to rob you of such riches in moments of weakness. Sometimes, they never come back. More than once, he has been caught out with plates in his room that have clearly been taken from St Peters without consent, an infringement which never fails to bring about a visit from the much-despised Mr Lord, the Executive Manager. The last time, a heated argument about inequality resulted in Wormwood losing the privilege of being taken out for the monthly outing.

This is what is known as a bad day. His room-mates are sensitive to these times and do their best to orientate him, though their own grasp of reality is a little less than reliable. He has become fixated with the notion that the room in which he sits is built on the remains of the burial site of Hereward the Wake. This has been the source of raging arguments with Amanda whose approach to these wild imaginings is not to indulge them but to rigidly insist that the residents remain as closely rooted in the present reality as possible. He imagines he is somehow linked to the perfectly preserved remains of the old rebel warrior who fought against the foreign invaders during the Norman Conquest. No doubt he sees a little something of himself in that defiant refusal to accept defeat and to rage against those who sought to impose their strange new ways on him and those under his protection.

In layers of clay, the old warrior now calls to him in a strange old dialect that he cannot quite understand. Whether the voice is telling him to come and dig him up or to give up the ghost and join him in eternity, Wormwood cannot say. But it disturbs him all the same.

'It's just the name of this stupid annex,' Amanda has told him before in her annoying schoolmistress voice. 'I suppose if you were next door in the Dickens Suite, you would imagine you were dictating 'Oliver Twist.'

His mind not being its usual quicksilver self, he resisted the temptation to quip that even Oliver wouldn't ask for more of the food he was routinely served up.

The voice is persistent, however; not hers, but that of the old warrior. Wormwood hears it in his sleep and he sometimes hears it during the day when his mind wanders, which it frequently does. The old bones rattle underground, agitated. Gold coins, jewel-encrusted weapons and a sumptuous helmet strain against the clay but are held fast.

'Back with us?' Wormwood has no idea what day it is, but James recognises a lucidity in his friend's eyes that tells him that his wits have returned.

'I guess so,' says Wormwood. He emerges from these states feeling quite revived. They are outside in the garden. 'What thrills have I missed?'

'Nothing much,' says James wistfully. 'It's Sunday. No visitors today, I'm afraid.'

'When did you ever know me to have a visitor?'

'I meant, for me. Sally hasn't made it today. Never mind.' It is something of a mystery. She never lets him down like this. To make matters worse, Ashok is obscured by loved ones fussing over him.

Wormwood is thirsty and eases himself up to go in search of a drink. Inside, out of the sun, he sees the boy sitting alone. He finds himself pleased to see him.

'You again.'

'Yup.'

'You must have been a naughty boy to be punished like this,' says Wormwood.

'Something like that.' The boy, Jake, looks like someone has drained him of energy, as if even the merest shrug takes an effort.

'Drink?'

'No thanks.' The boy shrugs.

'I meant, can you get me a drink. I'm thirsty.' Wormwood holds out a drained glass. 'I've been on a little journey.'

The boy takes the bait. 'Anywhere special?'

Wormwood taps his head. 'Here.'

The boy laughs. He has perfect little teeth. 'Time travel,' he says. 'Back to the past.'

'Maybe the future,' says Wormwood. 'I can't tell for sure.' The boy hands him a drink. They are comfortable in each other's company. 'Do you mind me asking? What exactly did you do?'

'It's a girl.' The boy's head goes down and a thick mass of tangled hair falls over his face.

'Of course it is,' says Wormwood. 'I wasn't always an old man, you know. I'll bet even your boring old grandad punched someone over some girl once upon a time.' He takes a long drink. 'So, what happened?'

'I was an idiot.' The boy's head droops. 'I thought I caught her with someone else.'

'So you punched him?' Wormwood indicates the boy's hand, which is in a plaster-cast. The boy shakes his head. 'You punched *her*? Bloody hell.'

'No, of course I didn't. I didn't punch anyone.' He turns his head away. 'I punched a wall.'

'The wall always wins.'

'Yeah, I pretty much learned that lesson. I wish I could talk to her, sort things out. But my mum went crazy and confiscated my phone. I can't stand not knowing.'

'We've all been there', says Wormwood, finishing his drink. 'Wait here.'

He struggles to his feet and returns a few moments later with a phone. 'Here.' He tosses it to the boy who catches it, barely.

The boy looks it over, incredulous. 'It's better than my phone,' he says. 'What the hell?'

'Do you mean thanks?' says Wormwood. 'It should have some charge. James never uses the damn thing.'

'Of course. Sorry. That's amazing.' Clearly using his wrong hand, clumsily, the boy has already called a number. Wormwood leaves him to it.

'What was that?' asks James, sitting a little hunched in the garden. He has a large puffy face from his medication, and his downturned mouth exacerbates his jowls. That said, he has a likeable face, honest and warm. His hair sits in grey wisps across his scalp.

'Women trouble.' They share a knowing grimace that resembles a smile. 'I let him use your phone.'

'Why not. I never use it anyway. I don't know why they got me the damn thing in the first place. I don't even know how to use it.'

'Guilt,' Wormwood suggests.

'Probably. Or that bloody son-in-law of mine trying to show off how successful he is.' It's not often that James talks like this. His daughter's absence has clearly got him concerned.

'You're not much of a fan of his,' says Wormwood.

'No, I'm not. I generally try to see the good in people, as you know, but in his case, I just can't see it.' A pair of garish butterflies distract him and he loses his train of thought. 'I always thought she would end up with someone a bit like me,' he goes on. 'We always got on so well. She clashed a bit with her mother when she was younger but we always saw the world in the same way.' Again, he drifts off into a little reverie, presumably recalling fond moments from their shared past. 'But this guy she has settled for, he's just such a braggart. Everything is a commodity to him, even Sally. Even his own children. Just something else to boast about, to make him look better.'

'Like buying you a state-of-the-art phone you can't even use.'

'Exactly. I think he got it for me to persuade her to come less often, so we can Skype, whatever the hell that is. I'm sure she would have moved me in with her, if it wasn't for him. She hates me being in here.' Wormwood just listens and nods in the right places. The boy walks over to them. His face is less of a dark scowl than previously as he hands the phone over to Wormwood, who shakes his head and gestures towards his friend.

'Oh,' he says, handing it back.

'Any better?' says James. 'Did it help?'

'I'm not sure,' he says uncertainly. 'She listened for a bit and then hung up. Thanks, anyway.'

'Sounds vaguely promising,' says Wormwood. 'I hope things work themselves out.'

'Yeah. I'd better be getting back.' He walks away and then comes back, looking sheepish. 'I almost forgot,' he whispers. 'I got you a present.' Surreptitiously, he reaches into a pocket and slips a joint into Wormwood's hand as they say goodbye.

Shortly thereafter, there is a bit of a commotion and the boy is brought back over to them by his mother, who looks less than overjoyed.

'Whose phone was it?' she demands brusquely.

'Good afternoon to you, too,' says Wormwood smartly. 'Is there a problem?'

She stands defiantly, fists on hips. 'Yes, there's a problem. This little shit tells me that someone let him use their phone when he knows damn well he's banned.'

'Oh,' says James awkwardly, 'That would have been —'

'—me,' Wormwood cuts in. 'That was my bright idea.'

'Well, thanks ever so much for undermining any authority I might have had.'

'I don't even know who you are,' says Wormwood calmly, never one to back down from a confrontation. 'I was getting to know the boy. He never asked to borrow the phone.' He meets her steely gaze. 'I offered. I like him.'

'Well, good for you. You don't have to live with him.'

'Lucky for him. He'd hate it here. He's smart.'

She sighs. 'Look', she says. 'You have no idea what's going in my life. All I ask is that you mind your own business and stop making it harder for me to exert any kind of control over this little —' She struggles to find the right word.

'I get the idea,' says Wormwood. No stranger to conflict, Wormwood is smart enough to know that sometimes the best way to win a fight is to stop swinging. 'Look. I'm just some poor old man stuck in the middle of hell on earth, I never get any visitors and your son kindly offered to pour me a drink on a hot day. We started to chat and hit it off. Where's the harm in that?'

She is wary. He is not what she expected to find in a place where people are effectively sent to stop being a nuisance. There is far too much vitality in his belligerence to explain why he is in stuck in the same place as the dried-up husk of her grandfather who she is here to visit out of a prolonged sense of familial obligation. He disarms her somewhat. 'No harm,' she says, taking the seat next to him. She places a hand on his arm. 'But why did you give him a phone?'

He sighs. 'Because the only way you ever learn how to deal with your problems—.' He pauses, suddenly a bit short of breath. He beckons her to sit down. '---is to deal with them.' He wipes his brow. 'Trust me on this one.' She sits. She is playing the game on his terms now.

'Okay,' she says. He can see that she is exhausted. The boy is not the start of her problems, but he might be the end of the rope as far as she is concerned. He has seen it before. 'Okay. He isn't talking to anyone else. If he will talk to you, great.' Her tone is far from upbeat. 'So be it.'

A dark angular shadow looms over them like some kind of German Expressionist ghoul. 'Is there a problem?' It is His Lordship, Mr Lord.

'Nope,' says Wormwood blithely. 'You can crawl back into your executive office. Everything is---.' He searches for the right phrase. 'Hunky dory.' Mr Lord looks at the boy's mother. He has a thin weak face and bulging eyes from high blood pressure. Despite the strain she is under, she retains that pretty glitter of latent beauty that has always alienated petty men and he clearly finds it hard to meet her gaze.

'All well?' he asks. His hands are clasped as if in a moment of religious contemplation, his eyes beseeching. Is he looking for the excuse?

'It's fine. This, erm, gentleman was just kindly offering some guidance to my son over there.' She nods vaguely to the left.

'Are you quite sure about that, madam?' There is dismay in the response.

She tries to return His Lordship's misdirected gaze but he is staring at her shoes. 'Yes. It's all fine. Thankyou. I know what I'm doing.' She rises. 'We're going,' she says, turning over her shoulder to address Wormwood. 'Thanks again for the chat. See you next week.'

'Already looking forward to it,' he says, smiling hideously at His Lordship as he does so. 'And off you scuttle, Mr Lord,' he says cheerily.

'You sure do love a good fight,' says Ashok later.

'Yes,' says Wormwood, 'I sure do.'

James is a little perplexed. 'But why do you always pick fights you can't win?' he asks. 'You're never going to beat Lord. He has all the power.' He is concerned about his friend who is clearly struggling to sit upright in his customary fashion. Wormwood is tired and his mind is starting to run on empty.

'Why?' he echoes, his voice a little weary. 'Because fights you can't win are the only ones worth fighting. Otherwise, you're just a bully.' He leans back and closes his eyes, imagining his good friend a few rooms away enjoying some much-needed herbal medication. A small victory, but a victory nonetheless.

Chapter 4

The next day Ashok is unwell. His cough has grown worse and his breathing has become more laboured and erratic so a doctor is called for. When the doctor finally arrives, he is sufficiently concerned for the staff to decide on a precautionary hospital visit and Ashok is taken away. His absence leaves a vacuum in the room. It is unseasonably hot and many of the residents are finding it a little difficult to catch their breath. The weather brings other problems, too, such as wasps. Immobile and generally made irresistible to flying pests by sticky fingers and traces of jam smeared across faces or lodged in beards, the residents are habitually bothered by wasps in particular. There is a device by the French doors that lead out to the garden that is designed to attract and eradicate them and James becomes fascinated by the macabre spectacle.

'I never understood what they were really for,' he says. 'Wasps, I mean.' A particularly large specimen narrowly avoids the heated elements of the killing machine. For someone who reads newspapers and generally makes an effort to try to understand why things happen, James is better at asking questions than discovering satisfactory answers.

'For all we know, they think much the same of us,' suggests Wormwood. 'Humans: what are we for? At least wasps don't destroy their own planet.' There has been another special report on the television that morning itemising the various ways in which humanity had plundered, poisoned and polluted and the natural world to the point of apocalypse.

'Yes, but they have a nasty sting,' says James. 'I mean, bees. They're busy. They make honey. I get that. But what purpose do wasps serve?' Wormwood is tempted briefly to attempt a philosophical discussion to help James on his noble course of self-improvement, but without Ashok he knows it will not end well.

'Humans do a lot worse than sting,' says Wormwood. He is going to elaborate on his comment but leaves it at that.

The wasp is back and finds itself caught on the element. It struggles but is held fast. In no special hurry, the device takes its times charring the wasp to a blackened husk, which ends in an electric zap.

'What if Ashok dies?' James wonders out loud. 'What if he doesn't come back?'

'Samsara,' says Wormwood. 'The circle of life and rebirth. He told you that already.'

'But it will be sad,' says James. 'To let him go like that.'

'For us, maybe. But not for him. This is hardly a life worth living, is it.' Wormwood gestures around him at their inelegant surroundings.

'Not so much, not anymore,' James agrees. 'But what if he comes back as a wasp?' Hence the obsession.

'I don't think you need to worry about that,' says Wormwood. 'I think he's been good enough to come back as something better than a bloody wasp.'

'Yes,' says James. 'Agreed.' He looks over at the chair where Ashok should be. 'He's a lovely man. I wish I knew him when he was younger. He's so—' As is often the case, he spends so long waiting for the right word to appear that he loses his thread. Wormwood plays a game in his head to fill in the gap. *Spiritual?* That's what people usually think of when it comes to India.

'Lucky,' said James, finally.

'Why lucky?'

'He's got so many people who love him. He says he's only in here because whoever got to look after him in his old age, it would cause hurt to the ones he didn't choose. Isn't that amazing?'

'Yes,' says Wormwood, patiently. 'It is amazing.' A butterfly enters the room and both men admire it. Whatever a wasp is, a butterfly is not. Gentle. Benevolent. Then James has a bad thought. Randomly, it nears the killing device. He struggles to his feet and waves a wooden stick to redirect it to safety. The spastic action creates a draft that has the opposite effect, pushing it upwards towards annihilation. Flapping with growing urgency as it senses the heat, the butterfly seems to have saved itself only to drift the wrong way. The vivid colours of its wing intensify as it convulses and bursts into a tiny flame.

'Bloody hell,' says James. He is visibly upset. 'Bloody hell.' Wormwood does his best to distract him but the day is ruined and he is forced to spend the rest of the afternoon in an awkward silence trying to imagine a better metaphor for the futility of existence.

James pours them all another glass of juice and that helps. There is little talk that evening. The TV is on the blink again and for the third night in a row there is no access to the news channels. Fortunately, they stumble across sports highlights and that does for them quite nicely.

Blissfully unaware of what is starting to unfold around them, another day slips into memory.

Where, exactly, does a story start and end? We are taught from our earliest days that a story is something that comes neatly packaged with a clearly delineated start - often signified by a neat phrase such as 'once upon a time' - followed by a properly sequenced order of events and then an educative ending that resolves with a helpful message or moral from which we can all learn how to make sense of the events unfolding around us and stay safe. As we become older and more experienced, we still try to see the world in these simplistic terms but come to appreciate that real life if a bit more complicated than that. It becomes harder to pin down exactly when a series of events started, and more problematic still to determine the sequence of events which led to a conclusion, and especially why those things happened. Like amateur detectives, we might try to work out the reasons why things played out in a certain way, and what alternative steps might have been taken to lead to a more satisfying conclusion. And as for that ending, we also need to work out what to make of it. Does it leave us sadder and wiser, as with the tale of the ancient mariner who shot the poor albatross, or filled with pathos at the fall of a great man with the tragic flaw? Do we seek closure to bring tragic events to a close for the common good, or vengeance for unspeakable injustices?

Take, for instance, the poor men waking up in a cold, sparsely furnished annex on the outskirts of an unfashionable city which is routinely mocked for its proximity to more wealthy and self-important cities to the east and south. We might ask ourselves what has brought them here. Like all things in life, there is no simple one-size-fits-all answer. In some cases, as with James, it is medical necessity, the care he requires being more than his family feel able to provide since he was widowed. There is no lack of love, merely, the lack of medical skill required to keep a failing body running through its routines to stay alive; in other cases economic hardship has forced a family with too few rooms to make the heart-breaking decision to leave their beloved in the hands of the state.

Wormwood coughs himself awake. Restful sleep has largely eluded him. He has spent the night in that dreadful half-sleep where anxieties warp into nightmare and it is hard to distinguish between what is real and what is not. He is quite confused. Were you to ask him how he has ended up in this state, he would struggle to spin a coherent narrative. His story is certainly no fairy tale, and it would be a disturbed child's mind that rendered a positive moral from the linear chronology of his life story from birth to the brink of the abyss in front of which he now stands on unsteady feet.

Let's see.

Abandoned by a mother as an infant in the aftermath of the last global war. Adopted by a military man of stern discipline and exacting standards. A problematic child, possibly quite brilliant though no one was sufficiently invested in him to discover in what way his talent might manifest itself. Insolent. Forced to abandon the freedoms which education might afford him in favour of a soldier's life to toughen him up. Haunted by the spectre of a life he might have enjoyed. Finally broken by two tours of Ireland that leave his life shattered. This is not a neat triangle of a story with leading to a happy resolution through a series of trials but a nebula of plot points that only a genius/ madman could draw into any kind of meaningful constellation - the broken man, the drifter...

Finally, the night swallows him and he finds sleep, or it finds him.

Chapter 5

'Where's Ashok?' he demands upon waking. There is no one in the room. The demons of the night are still in his mind. 'What's happening to him?' He sees a face in the window, an ancient face drawn with worry, a face that has nearly given up hope despite the crown that sits lopsided upon its brow. He stares at the face and sees his own face in it. Agitated, he calls out again. This time, James answers.

'It's okay,' he says reassuringly. 'You've had a nightmare, that's all.' He smiles weakly at his friend.

'But I'm awake,' says Wormwood. 'I'm wide awake and the nightmare is still here. Where's Ashok?'

'I'm sure he's in good hands,' says James, though there is a wobble to his voice. 'He'll be fine. He'll be back soon. You'll see.'

But the longer the day wears on, there is nothing good to see. No news is bad news and Wormwood becomes increasingly agitated, more of a nuisance than normal. Amanda isn't in and Wormwood almost misses her when he is informed that she is unlikely to be in work for some time. Her replacement is from an agency and barely speaks a word of English. As such, she is not able to satisfy any of Wormwood's requests for more information. Finally, exasperated, the staff strap him to a chair and take him away.

His Lordship's office is grander than it has any right to be when the money used to furnish it might have been better allocated elsewhere. Though there is nothing in the way of personal touches, every item of furniture is of the highest quality and corporate good taste, no doubt designed to impress the paying client that their loved ones are being passed over into capable hands. Wormwood has been here before numerous times. He is more lucid now. The day has been kind to him in this one small way; it would not do to be summoned to his Lordship's office when his blade has been blunted.

'So, here we are again, Mr Wormwood,' he says to open the proceedings. When he speaks, he has the unfortunate habit of twisting the corner of his mouth a little and it serves to make him sound insincere. 'I understand you are a little upset today. But it won't do, Mr Wormwood, disturbing the peace and abusing the staff.' He places his hands together as if in prayer, 'There are things going on of which you can have no comprehension. We have better things to do right now than deal with your little...' He searches vainly for the right word.

'Protest?' says Wormwood. 'Consider me a campaigner for social justice, fighting for the rights of the individual and all that.'

'I was thinking brat fit.' Lord sits back, satisfied he has found the word he is reaching for.

'Look,' says Wormwood, opting for a more direct approach. 'We are concerned. We have a right to know what has happened to Ashok. That's all.' As he was pushed around the complex, he couldn't help but notice the amount of unusual activity taking place, nothing he could put his finger on exactly, but certainly things which were not part of the usual routines and protocols of such an establishment. 'We just want to know what's going on.'

'I'm afraid you'll have to be more precise.'

'Something here. Something out there. Something you're not telling us. Fewer visits. The food is getting worse, if such a thing is possible.' As he articulates his concerns, a window is opening up in his mind. The speed with which they came to take Ashok away. The faces of the staff when they took him. The gloves. The masks. 'Something isn't right.'

'I can assure you that your friend is fine.' When Mr Lord smiles, you are put in mind of a demon from a Bosch painting, such is the absence of warmth. 'He is in good hands. He is in the local hospital on a ventilator, getting the treatment he needs.'

Wormwood is silent, contemplative, his mind trying to put pieces together with no clear sense of the whole picture.

'Another thing I need to raise with you is those awful horror films you insist on watching.'

'Yes,' says Wormwood. 'What about them?'

'There have been a number of complaints about them. They're hardly appropriate viewing in a setting like this, are they.' It is a rhetorical question.

'There have not been any complaints,' Wormwood corrects him. 'The others love them, too. The only person they upset is Nurse Amanda, and she doesn't have to watch them. And by extension, you are upset by them, too, I suppose, as she no doubt comes scuttling into your inner sanctum moaning about how offended she is. So, to sum up, what you are in fact saying is that two people are indirectly upset by something they don't have to watch.'

'But you to see that they are grossly inappropriate for this kind of residential setting.' Mr Lord likes to reiterate each point he makes. He thinks it makes him seem emphatic. 'I can't imagine what anyone could find to enjoy about them.'

'I like the simple binary narrative,' he explains. 'There are good people and there is evil. And they battle it out, and you know who everyone is and what they stand for.'

'What's so good about that?'

'Because that's how I would like real life to be. I want people to try to be good, and I want to be able to easily recognise evil so we know who and what to fight. Whereas what in fact happens is that good people get squashed by the system and evil hides behind corporate desks making soulless decisions that harm other people.'

'I am hardly evil, Mr Wormwood, and you are hardly what we might call a good person.' Lord makes a bizarre noise which he must imagine resembles a laugh. 'I'm just a busy man trying to do his job as well as he can to allow people to live with dignity.'

'And die quietly, out of sight and out of mind.'

'That is a little bit melodramatic, don't you think? Caring for the elderly is a messy business in every sense of the word. It is often not nice and certainly not pretty and there is little room for sentimentality. Someone has to make the hard decisions. I don't expect you to like it or to see things from my point of view, but there we have it.'

'Maybe so, but I am still not prepared to give up my films. They are a small glimmer of excitement in our otherwise dull lives,' says Wormwood with a smile. 'And they keep us awake at night afterwards, which is great.'

Lord takes the bait. 'And why is that so great?'

'Because the more we are awake, the longer we stay alive. What would you suggest we watch? 'Songs of Praise', perhaps? We're not of that generation that just sat there and died with a stiff upper lip.' He has become quite animated. 'The war we fought in was the one against the establishment. We were the mods and we were the rockers. We were the students protesting on the streets. We expanded our minds and changed the world. Remember, we're the ones who put the BOOM! in boomer.'

His Lordship is distinctly unimpressed. 'I thought you said that life here was intolerably boring?'

'Finally,' says Wormwood. 'At last you're seeing things from my perspective.'

There is a long deliberate sigh. 'Let me be blunt. I never wanted you here, Mr Wormwood. You are a trouble-maker and a drain on our resources. I have warned you before god knows how many times about your attitude to the staff and myself. Be warned. It is better in here than it is out there.' He violently jerks a thumb towards the window.

'Do you mean I am free to go, if I want?' says Wormwood. 'Believe me, I have no desire to stay in here a second longer than I need to be.' He makes a pantomime of getting up to go.

'Sit down. We both know you are not permitted to leave. We have a legal duty of care towards you and I have absolutely no intention of ruining my career over someone such as yourself.' His voice has become more irritable than he intended.

Wormwood settles down. Slowly, he slides back and makes himself more comfortable. 'I'm starting to think you don't like me. Have I done something to upset you?'

'Everything you do upsets me,' Lord readily admits, abandoning any attempt at civility. 'I read your file before I agreed to take you. Why would you think I would want someone like you here making things difficult? Virtually homeless. An ex-convict. A dishonoured man.' He spat the words like they contained traces of poison.

'And yet,' says Wormwood, 'at least out there I didn't have to put up with sanctimonious little pricks like you.'

'Well, there we have it.' He smirks, his mouth twisting up on itself. 'If we are going to speak so bluntly to one another, let's have at it, shall we.'

He sits forward, props his elbows on his mahogany desk, his fingers casually touching at the tips. In the distance, an ambulance siren howls. 'Your friend? Let's just say he isn't likely to be coming back any time soon. I am sorry to have to tell you that he is far more ill than we believed.'

'You're not sorry at all.'

'Oh, but I am.' He disagrees. 'I am sorry. I'm really quite sorry for your friend and all his family. I just don't care a jot about you.'

Wormwood's hands grip the arms of the chair until his knuckles turn white. 'One day', he snarls, 'I'm going to make you feel very sorry for yourself, you little turd.'

'Yes, I've read your file, remember?' He twists the knife. 'I know exactly what you are capable of, old man, when someone gets under your skin. But as it happens, you are right. Something is coming, and you're not going to like it. Let's just see what happens next, shall we.' He pushes a button on his desk and an orderly comes to take Wormwood away, his curses fading into the long evening, as much in frustration at letting his nemesis get the better of him than concern over what has happened to his good friend.

Later, when he has calmed down a little, James asks him if he has learned anything, and he keeps it to himself.

'Just a routine spell on the naughty step', he says. But when his head hits the pillow and searches for oblivion, all he can hear is the sound of machinery whirring in his head, albeit cogs and wheels in desperate need of oil.

Chapter 6

The next few days pass by unremarkably, although the calm is deceptive as there is a noticeable reduction in the services. No-one appears to help the immobile move outside and it is left to the more able clients such as Wormwood and James to help move people around. Mealtimes are less rigid than normal. On Friday, dinner is served almost two hours late. There are no hairdresser appointments. Calls on the red emergency button go largely unheeded. Outside, there appears to be a lot of activity going on but inside quite the opposite is true. Routine is both a prison and the key that unlocks it; it is a source of comfort to those whose lives are otherwise an indistinguishable cycle of monotony, but it also leads to a level of dependency which is distinctly unhealthy.

For those in the Annex, it is like one of those dreams we all have when we are trapped behind a glass wall and no one can hear you. They are becoming fossilised. The less there is to do, the less able they feel to do anything for themselves. Even Wormwood is unnaturally quiet, though he notices that their medication is not always as it should be in terms of dosage and even the colours of the pills. If and when they put in an appearance, the staff inform him that there has been a slight issue with the supply chains and that they are being given alternative brands. Never one to take things at face value, like all thinking men, Wormwood is unconvinced, although there is a fog in his head that makes it hard to thread a clear path from A to B. Paranoid that he is being doped, he stops taking his medication altogether, and starts to feel more like his old self almost immediately. On Thursday, they are informed by agency staff that there will be no visits at the weekend. Their demands for more information are met with a wall of indifference. Hopefully, they are told, things will be back to normal next week.

But that seems increasingly unlikely. It transpires that Ted died in the night, no one with him to hold his hand, mop his brow or tell him things were going to be okay, to support him in the transition from one state of being to the next. Two workers turn up in mid-morning and wheel him away in his bed. They are unable to answer any questions, capable of conversing only in a pidgin hybrid of very crude English and an East European language which is hard to pin down or decipher.

'Poor bloody sod,' says James. 'What a way to go.' Judging by the smell of him and the lack of care he has received, the men are not convinced that he hasn't lain dead for several days. When Wormwood demands to see His Lordship, he is told in broken English that the big boss man is far too busy. When he kicks off, he is unceremoniously strapped to his bed where he lies fuming for half a day before he is relieved.

Once upon a time, it was inconceivable that one of the richest countries in the planet could treat its senior citizens in such a brutal manner. But on the sabbath, on visiting day no less, the wheels stop turning and everything grinds to a stop. No care workers march brusquely through the doors to wake them up. Not only is there no sign of breakfast, there is not even the distant clatter of pans that signify that food is being prepared. When red buttons are pressed repeatedly to call for help, none if forthcoming. The silence, as they say, is deafening.

Wormwood wakes up heavily. The night has once again been unforgiving. He feels as though he is starting to live his life in rewind, replaying significant events in his life as in a silent film, events which for the most part he would have preferred not to have lived through the first time. As morning light filtered into his nightmares, his visions shifted. He heard the loud beating of metal against metal, like ancient warriors psyching themselves up for battle, though as he awoke, it transpires that what he could hear is his own pulse throbbing in his temples.

'What day is this?' he asks.

James shrugs. 'Let's call it day one,' he suggests. 'There's no one here.'

'We're here.'

Fortunately, James is immune to Wormwood's earl morning moods. 'Yes, we are. But there are no staff. If I didn't know any better, I would say we have been...abandoned to our own care.'

'You mean left to rot?' Wormwood's voice is more like an animalistic growl.

'Well, that is another way of putting it.' James actually manages some kind of jaunty laugh as if this is some kind of grand adventure. Before his mind can start to ask of itself if this is the start of the end, James automatically switches into positivity. 'Come on, get some clothes on, I need some coffee.' While Wormwood struggles into his day clothes, James tries the TV but, like the radio, it hasn't worked for several days as if someone had fiddled with the external aerial or some kind of apocalyptic event has befallen the world. Overnight, the digital world has been replaced by static hiss or, worse, silence.

As they make their way through the Annex, they check quickly on the other inmates and reassure them that coffee, at the very least, will shortly be putting in an appearance, so that some sort of normal service might be resumed to quiet grumbling bellies and reassure some of the more anxious amongst them.

'Any chance of more weed?' asks Windrush. 'That was a nice touch, my friend.'

Wormwood smiles. 'Not today,' he says, 'But I can offer you some caffeine if you like. I'll even roll it up into a joint and you can smoke it, if you prefer.'

Windrush laughs, a great booming sound that generally ends in a coughing fit, his lungs shredded long ago. 'A mug will do just fine.'

Coffee makes everything better, apart from the throbbing in Wormwood's head. He assumes it is the anger that has overwhelmed him upon waking up to discover the callous manner in which they have been abandoned. Though he feels far from helpless, even the short walk from their room to the kitchen has revealed not only the full extent to which they are alone, but also the number of people who are now effectively dependent upon what little care he is able to provide. All around, there are clear signs that the place has been deserted at very short notice. Food has been left in fridges and freezers and there is sufficient milk to make a full round of morning beverages, for today at least. The phones have been disconnected; at the very least, the line is dead when James lifts the receiver and tries to call out. He tries to press 0 for an outside line, with the same result. All lines of communication are dead. Windrush, who has joined them for some exercise, shakes his head, his grey dreadlocks rattling as he does so.

'Let me try,' says Wormwood, stretching out an arm. He calls the emergency services and strains to hear a response. The effect is like a putting a seashell to your ear in that after a few seconds all he can hear is the steady whoosh of his own pulse. Frustrated, he smashes the receiver against a worktop.

'Great,' says James, avoiding his friend's glare. 'That will help.' They pile mugs of tea and coffee onto a tray and start their rounds, after which they are exhausted

'What now?' says James, as they finally sit and drink their own brews. He is used to deferring to Wormwood.

'Wait,' says Wormwood. 'I am thinking.' He summons the energy to consider all the facts he has before him and tries to sort them into something that will provide him with the means to weigh up his options and formulate some kind of plan. As James waits, Wormwood starts to look all of his seventy-three years. Finally, he comes to.

'I need more information. We need to go to the other side. They left in a hurry. There must be something that will help us to discover what the hell is going on. Until we know what is going on, there is no way of knowing how best to proceed.'

James nods. 'Knowledge is power', he agrees. But it is not that easy. When they try the door to the other side, they discover to their dismay that they have been locked in. Locked out. James has the presence of mind to try his mobile phone again, but there is no signal and the messenger services are also out of service.

In some ways, it is the best thing that could have happened. Wormwood is enervated by the affront to his liberty. He surveys the lock like a master criminal, considering options. As he struggles with various tools he has selected to try to force the lock, the creases that scar his face seem to fall away. Sweat turns his greying hair darker. Finally, with several mighty swings of a hammer, he bludgeons the handles and is able to withdraw the lock so that the door can be forced open.

'The game is afoot,' he says melodramatically, and steps through into the other side. Every door has been locked, but Wormwood is able to locate a master key which has been carelessly tossed aside in the rush to abandon ship. Perhaps the most significant thing they are able to discover is the most glaring one of all - each of the residents of St Peters has been removed. Most of their belongings have been left behind in the haste to get them to whatever safety lies outside these walls that have become their home for however long, but the fact remains that they have been spirited away whilst others, such as James and Wormwood, have been left to whatever pathetic demise fate had in store for them.

For one already possessed with a naturally dim view of his fellow man, Wormwood's reaction is damning. His head drops briefly. 'Bastards,' he says. It is barely a whisper, a curse meant for no one in particular, just a general summing up of the morning's state of affairs. He finds that the master key does not work in His Lordship's office, but he and Windrush put their shoulders to the door and eventually it gives.

Half-heartedly, they turn it upside down in search of anything that might come in useful, but all they really manage to discover is the lack of any personal clutter pertaining to its former resident. The most damning thing they discover is a half-eaten bar of chocolate.

'He really is one boring son of a bitch,' says Windrush. 'No wife. No kids.'

'No mistress,' says Wormwood. 'In fact, no life at all.' At a nurse's station they do find a book which itemises all phone calls they have received from loved ones. There is a noticeable rise in the recent days, maybe four or five times the usual amount. James' daughter alone had called seven times in the previous 24 hours before the nurses and care workers stopped bothering to record details. They try the front doors and discover – to little surprise – that they are locked.

'They've gone and caged us in,' says Windrush. 'Like animals. That's not right.'

They spend several minutes trying to force the doors, then check the windows and all other possible means of escape. With little anticipation of success, they locate tools that might be used to smash a window and spend what little strength they have left, all to no avail. They retire to the relative comfort of His Lordship's office and take stock.

'Damn it,' says Windrush. 'What next, big man?'

Wormwood picks up a glass paperweight on the desk and launches it against a far wall where it happens to catch a framed certificate full on. It disintegrates into a thousand tiny splinters and shards.

'Did that help?' asks James.

'I don't know yet.' From where he is seated, Wormwood can see himself in the destroyed remnants of the frame. He is struck by the reflection of himself in the shattered glass, like a fragmented portrait that Picasso might have painted. It is as though he is seeing a new version of himself being composed, not the useless old man that others had come to see him as but as something else. Through what appears to be nothing more than a petulant act of violence, perhaps what he can now see staring defiantly back at him is some kind of evolution of the man he had become. He is quiet, contemplative. He has become accustomed to self-doubt, unsure whether his translucent thinking is a result of crudely-administered medication, the dreaded early onset of the great memory thief, or... something else.

Windrush is not happy. 'This is bad,' he says. 'This is really bad'.

'But it doesn't have to be,' says Wormwood. His voice is a little uncertain, as if he is still in the process of fully gathering his true thoughts. 'Look around,' he says. 'Yesterday, we couldn't even have dreamed that they would just clear off and leave us in peace. There was not even the slightest notion that anything was going to happen that would change the way we see out our last days. We knew how it was going to be. Days blurring into an endless cycle of boredom, frustrated hopes and growing discomfort, then pain and more pain,'

'Is this supposed to give me hope?' asks Windrush, but there is an unmistakable glint in his eyes as he allows his friend to continue.

'Look at it this way,' says Wormwood. 'Any sense of who we used to be was stripped away from us as soon as we arrived, no more than three personal possessions and all that rubbish. We had to let petty little bureaucrats govern our hours, we were stripped of any sense of dignity one little piece at a time, and then we did the decent thing and gave up the ghost. That was the best we could hope for. A quick, quiet death. Hoping you have the courage to face up to that moment in the night when the breath catches in your throat, or your lungs fill up, or you feel the blow-out in your brain that finally stops the clock.' He looks at his old friend. 'You know what I'm talking about, he says. 'We all know it's coming.'

'And now?'

'Now? We're free,' says Wormwood.

'Free?' Are you having a bad spell or something, old man? We can't even get out.'

Wormwood struggles to his feet and gestures expansively. 'True,' he says, 'But we have everything we need right here. It's all just a matter of perspective. We could just sit here crushed by the inevitability of our impending doom, which to be honest doesn't sound very appealing, or we could decide to view this as an amazing opportunity to make some changes.'

'Glass half full,' says Windrush, nodding in agreement. 'I like it.'

They make up the rest as they go along, moving from room to room in the Annex and spreading the good news. Indolence makes idiots of us all, but given a job to do, the change that sweeps over Peterloo is extraordinary. With Wormwood as leader and James and Windrush his trusted lieutenants, the place is transformed. For starters, Windrush commandeers the intercom system and soon music is blasting out loudly enough so that even the most hard of hearing can feel the bass booming through their ribcage. Former cooks volunteer to make note of what is left in the larders and freezers and immediately get to work preparing a meal. James takes over a medical role, based on first aid courses he took when he was a useful member of society trying to keep idiots from electrocuting themselves in their homes. He is methodical in his work, carefully itemising what medication they can locate and working out what everyone's specific needs are, though his medical knowledge is best described as primitive. He agrees with Wormwood that they are to stop administering sedatives forthwith, especially when it is discovered that Wormwood has been placed on an alarmingly high dosage for months without him knowing. Within hours, some who have been bed-ridden for months are unsteadily up on their feet and participating as best they can in the general melee.

Not everyone is swept along with the sudden mood of frivolity. Some are too institutionalised to be able to let go of the safety rope; some literally pull the covers over their heads and try to sleep through it, whilst there are several residents who are too far over the brink to make it back. They state at Windrush as if it is Death himself who has appeared at their bedside to urge them to throw off their shackles and join the party. Their faces stricken with a look of horror, James does his level best to cater for them and then they are pretty much left to it.

That evening, however, considerably more than half of the residents of the Annex totalling over twenty people, eat altogether in a communal space which has been laid out by residents who had previously worked in hospitality. They have all dressed up in their finest and are determined to make the most of it while it lasts. Some literally look decades younger. Wormwood, for example, has helped himself to a fine linen suit from the room he has requisitioned. He has washed his hair and fashioned it into something that resembles respectability, for once.

'You look very handsome tonight,' he is informed by one of the female residents. She is wearing an elegant silk dress in turquoise that offsets her auburn hair.

'And you, madam, look very beautiful.' He can be quite the gentleman when the mood takes him, it would appear.

'Be careful, my friend. A man of your age...' Windrush likes to tease him. He has tactically seated himself next to her.

'No fear of that,' says Wormwood. 'I gave all that up years ago.'

They eat better than they can ever remember; in truth the food is not great, though the fault is not with those preparing it but the poverty of ingredients. What gives it such extraordinary flavour is the taste of freedom and the intense satisfaction of having been useful. They enjoy getting to know each other, allowing themselves to become something of the person they once were, not who dire circumstance or the unforgiving inevitability of age has condemned them to become.

Windrush suggests to Wormwood that he should give a speech. Politely, he declines.

'Why me?' he protests. 'I'm no leader. That's not who I am.'

'Make a speech, white man,' says Windrush

Wormwood shakes his head. 'I'm no public speaker,' he says.

James smiles warmly at him. 'You could have fooled me,' he says. 'You never bloody shut up.'

Reluctantly, he stands up to a warm round of applause. Like all people who are too smart for their own good, when faced with an expectant audience - in this case quite literally a captive audience - he discovers he has nothing to say.

'I don't know what you want me to say,' he says, turning into a blind alley. He understands that what they probably want to hear is something inspirational, something life-affirming but that is not who he is and he is not one to be fraudulent with his feelings. 'I want to say thank you to the people who prepared this amazing feast. It's been quite a day.'

'Amen to that,' says Windrush.

'But let's not fool ourselves. The fact that we have been abandoned here is an outrage.' Looking down for a moment, he discovers his fists are clenched. 'If there is any justice left in the world, heads should roll for this. You deserve better than this. We may not know what is going on out there, but it doesn't matter if it's nuclear war or a zombie plague: any society that allows its elderly to rot to death cannot consider itself civilised.' He has put aside his fury all day in an attempt to mitigate the fear and anxiety that otherwise would have overwhelmed them, but he can no longer contain it. 'To badly paraphrase something a wise man once said, I for one am not prepared to go quietly into the night. All I know is how to fight. And that's just what I'm going to do.'

He tries to meet all their gazes. This is not quite what they were expecting, but he certainly has their attention. What else did they expect? This, after all, is Wormwood, that great malcontent, scourge of the petty bureaucrat, arch-defender of those weaker than himself. They have all had to listen to him rant and rave against any perceived slight or injustice, never a backward foot taken unless – as in the case of Windrush – it was likely to cause greater injury to someone about whom he cared.

'So,' he continues, 'it seems we have been written off. We are just a tiny pathetic footnote in the future history of whatever misfortune has overtaken us. Well, that may be so, but that doesn't mean we have to go down without a fight. Needing help is not the same as being helpless.' Though they are hermetically sealed in behind sealed double-glazed units, he can smell the ancient soil all around, a layer of clay which has protected the remains of chieftains and warriors who have fought more noble causes than this, and against greater odds. They have found cheap boxes of wine stored for a staff party and they now manage to raise a toast in plastic cups.

'Raise a glass, my friends,' he says. 'I am glad that you partied today like it is your last day on earth. Let's face it, if we don't get help soon, it may well be our last day. But at the very least we can go out fighting.'

When he has finished, they manage to raise a cheer and, apparently having heeded his words, do what they can to make the most of it, though all but Wormwood and James are fast asleep long before midnight.

'Bloody hell,' says James. 'I never thought it was going to end like this.'

'Weren't you listening?' says Wormwood. They are sitting next to each other on a sofa. 'This isn't the end.'

'What's this,' says James. He is drunk and his voice slurs like a bad actor. 'Another inspirational/ depressing speech?'

'No, just the truth. This is not the end,' He laughs darkly, to himself. 'It's just the start of the end. Anyway, it was your sodding idea,' says Wormwood. 'I was quite happy just to get pissed.'

'You did okay,' says James.' Did you ever think of going into politics?' He is not even half-serious.

'If I had,' says his friend, 'I think I would have been shot for sedition.'

'Hanged.'

'Same difference, you pedant.'

They are so tired they can barely speak. 'Thanks for today,' says James. 'I mean it. All my life I've tried to be good, to be part of the consensus, kept my mouth shut, and look where's it's got me.'

Wormwood looks around. It is fair to say Peterloo is not looking its finest; this is not an image that would make its way into the next glossy brochure, should there be one.

'Today should have been the worst day of our lives,' says James, summoning the effort to speak through sheer will.

'Believe me, I've had worse,' says Wormwood.

'But that's the point. You made it okay. I had a great day, actually.' He drains his glass. 'It was the best day most of us had had in a long time. You made it happen. Whatever happens next, I want you to know that I'll be with you.'

'It's going to be tough,' says Wormwood, 'but that means a lot.' The old men embrace each other, already looking like the ghosts into which they are about to metamorphose. A moon has come up and illuminates the scene with brilliant clarity. Its pull is gently fierce, invisibly drawing the essence of rebellion out of the clay on which Peterloo itself has been constructed, as ephemeral as the residents who have now mostly fallen asleep inside its uPVC walls. For now at least, a kind of peace has descended. Somewhere a fox screams like a baby and countless layers of earth crush waste matter into diamonds.

Chapter 7

Wormwood is the first to rise the next morning. It is a terrible cliché to say that someone feels like death warmed up after a night's hard drinking, but on this occasion it is an apt phrase. He senses the presence of death all around him, not with the dread that compels the young to hide under their bedcovers; this embodiment of Death is the hyena that steadily follows at an amoral trot, the vulture that circles in slyly descending circles. The romantic notion of the previous evening that they were going to carry on fighting regardless of their circumstances has quickly dissipated. The air is foul with the stench of people who are unaccustomed to toileting without support. Unsteady on his feet, Wormwood first goes in search of water, perhaps even the possibility of caffeine. Having slept on the sofa where he fell last night, he has lost his bearings and even finds himself stumbling along a wall as if he has recently been blinded. Some leader, this. Some warrior king.

Eventually, he locates the kitchen and a tap. He drinks deeply, pouring the third cup over his head. He fills the kettle and finds a cup, his hand visibly trembling as he measures instant coffee granules and sugar into a mug emblazoned with the corporate logo, Caveo. His mouth is horribly dry but he spits into the cup, a small gesture of defiance. He slumps into a chair and enjoys the drink as it revives him. His mind tries to determine his next course of action, but it somehow feels disconnected from himself. There is much work to be done, and he is well aware that he might not be equal to the tasks that lie ahead. Placing his hands on his thighs, he rises again, allowing himself time to get his bearings. Someone somewhere is calling out for assistance. Others begin to stir. Wormwood has not looked at a clock, but a weak sun stretches shadows across the room as he heads off, informing him that it is still early. Better to sleep, but it is what it is. The pleading voice summons him. On the way, he stumbles into a room to find Windrush making the beast with one of the female residents. whose name is Rebecca, she of the turquoise dress. Their rhythmic movements are barely perceptible. Her head has rolled back onto the pillow, her eyes like tiny diamonds.

He finds Arthur covered in his own filth. 'I'm so sorry,' he says again and again, as Wormwood heaves him up and does his best to clean him, ruining his crumpled suit in the process. There are plenty more where it came from.

'We've all been there,' he says. 'No need to apologise.' What he means of course is the fault lies not with this poor old man who has lost his ability to self-maintain but the authorities who have been derelict in their duties. Once a semblance of dignity has been restored, he leaves an exhausted Arthur to it and sets off to do a round of the Annex.

It is a truly a horror show. After the first death, once the first corpse has been discovered in their bed, shrouded in a Caveo-branded blanket, there can be no hiding from the reality that faces them. There is no bravado-inducing speech that can distract from the dark fact that they are alone and abandoned. Death is no stranger to this place, for sure, but he has always been an unwelcome if frequent visitor; now uPVC doors have been thrown open and he has been invited in.

In all, three residents have not made it through the long night. Everyone is now awake, after a fashion. Some are decidedly groggy. Though a little diminished by his morning's exercise, Windrush is up to the task of helping James and Wormwood first of all locate implements which might function as spades and then helping to dig impromptu graves in the small garden at the centre of the complex, encircled by the rest of the buildings. A horrible stench of filth now pervades every room and space. The ground is hard and they barely get down sufficiently deep to lay in the bodies, and by the time they have finished covering them with dirt, the graves extend some distance from the ground level. Still, it is enough to afford them a little dignity.

Rebecca has fashioned crude crosses out of a wooden chair broken the previous evening, and with Wormwood's assistance she now places them respectfully on each mound of earth. Windrush scatters some earth over the mounds as Wormwood automatically intones prayers to send them peacefully on their way to wherever it is they are going next.

'Are you a believer?' Rebecca asks him when the rites are finished. It is clear that she knows little about him. If he were a polite man, he would tell her that he was so she might take comfort in the mumbled jumbled prayers he has just offered, but that is not who he is.

His head is still lowered. 'I believe in nothing,' he says.

'That's not strictly true,' she responds. 'You're a good friend. I can see that. And you try to do the right thing.'

'For all the good it does anybody.' He is in a bleak mood today, though fate has given him little reason to be anything other.

'At least you still try,' she says. She smiles at him. She has a warm face and would have been quite a beauty in her day. A cold breeze causes them to shiver but they are reluctant to go back inside to face the reality that awaits them.

'I always wanted to sleep with a black guy,' she says to him conspiratorially. It doesn't even occur to him that it's the first time he has heard her speak. 'I loved my husband but he's years dead and buried. I know he wouldn't mind. What difference does it make now, eh.' There is no good answer; in truth, it was not intended as a question, merely a statement of fact. Wormwood doesn't really know how to respond, so he places his hand across the top of her head. Again, it doesn't occur to him that from the outside looking in his action somewhat resembles what Jesus might have looked like when he blessed sinners, if the son of God had been a heavily built man of seventy-three dressed in what can loosely be called lounge wear.

As the most pragmatic and capable amongst them, it falls to James to devise an immediate plan of action. Breakfast. The priority has to be keep going. The power and water supply is still functioning normally, so it is at least theoretically possible to keep the residents cleaned and fed. If the stench is not brought under some kind of control, life will soon become intolerable, and their collective health will rapidly decline. The decision is made collectively for those who are able to support the more needy, and then do their best to clean themselves afterwards.

Wormwood only agrees when James points out the obvious to him.

'I thought you would have approved,' he teases. 'It's Marxism in action. From each according to his ability; to each according to his need.' Wormwood stops short of saying out loud that such fine sentiments are admirable, but not when your back is breaking; he certainly thinks it, though. For one who is quite enlightened in much of his thinking, he is like many of his political anti-heroes in still being very much a man of his age. Cleaning up shit is no work for a man, he grumbles to himself. Hereward the Woke he is not.

After a hard morning of cleaning and self-care, rewarded at least with a decent breakfast, Wormwood has the bright idea of relocating to the more illustrious rooms on the other side of the building. Perhaps his morning's exertions have put something of the Bolsheviks storming the Winter palace into his way of thinking.

'Feather pillows,' he says, temptingly. In truth, he has no idea if the bedding in St Peters is as luxurious as he sells it to the others, but the rooms are unquestionably bigger and better-appointed in every conceivable way, and they have the added advantage that they have not yet been spoiled with human waste. Those who are bed-ridden grumpily refuse to move, but most people join Wormwood in his proposed resettlement, albeit one that takes mere minutes to accomplish. Before he opens the doors to their new home, he proudly proclaims: 'Welcome to the Promised Land.' The jubilation in his voice is at least partly prompted by the thought of what Nurse Ratshit's face would look like if she knew, as well as the anticipation of a well-earned sleep for the rest of the afternoon.

'Are you sure this is okay?' asks Rebecca.

'Who is there to stop us?' says Windrush, pushing her through. They waste a happy afternoon allocating rooms, sleeping and trying out their enhanced facilities before more serious matters have to be attended to. Back in Peterloo, two more residents are seriously ill. Though one or two people have basic medical knowledge, this is beyond their jurisdiction. Wormwood's back still aches from the effort of scraping out three erstwhile graves earlier that day and is in no hurry to push himself any further. He retires to Lord's office to test the phones again, in case the service has been miraculously reconnected.

On a whim, he thinks to tip out the bin, hoping to discover a clue to unlock the mystery of why they have been left to die alone. Of course, he already knows the reason, that some misfortune has stricken the country and hard economic and practical decisions have been made for the common good. Old people are functionless and burdensome in time of crisis. To abandon them makes some kind of Malthusian sense in terms of allocating resources to deal with the crisis as efficiently as possible. This is no time for sentimentality; the time has come for common sense to prevail. To the Caveo stakeholders, a few dozen pensioners are acceptable collateral damage. Wormwood has met their kind before, and he has never come out of it well. Why should this time be any different?

Exhausted, numbed, he stares out of the window across a landscape that will never grace a biscuit tin. On the horizon, the silhouette of a cathedral signifies a setting sun. It was always hard for him to believe in the existence of a benevolent being; now it is downright impossible. He instinctively understands that the concept of civilisation was a thinly painted lacquer that was used to paint over defects and blemishes. Easily scratched, a flimsy inadequate layer hiding a horrible truth. The stench permeates through the closed door but what causes Wormwood to retch and gag is not the smell but the realisation that dignity is a self-deluding myth.

Returning to the others, he is informed that food supplies are running low, although they have located enough medication to see them through the worst of it. He understands that the phrase that James chooses to use is skilfully coded. The stocks of pills will outlast them all. Windrush selects another CD from his collection and plays reggae at rib-cracking volumes which is absurdly incongruous in every conceivable way and lends a surreal and unintentionally darkly comic tone to the unfolding drama. They make the collective decision to eat well that evening and then begin a system of rationing thereafter, the argument being that they require energy to maintain their strength to carry out their responsibilities to their fellow residents and fight off the fatigue that is starting to overwhelm them. James masks his concern at Wormwood's increasingly haunted expression and directs the others to prepare another meal, leaving Wormwood who has made the mistake of sitting down and within moments has sunk into oblivion.

He dreams that the delightful deep-clean lady is outside banging on a window. She has baked for them, exquisitely decorated little cakes. Her lovely face is stretched into a beatific smile, but as she rests her palms on the windows, he sees that she is also crying. Tears roll down her face. Behind her, the last of the sun is pulled down beyond the horizon and a halo is cast around her. The vision is more vivid as it comes at the moment shortly before wakefulness, in that hinterland between dream and reality.

He wakes with a start. There actually is banging at the window, and a face. It is, of all the unlikeliest people, Amanda. She is banging as hard as she dares against the window.

'It's you,' he says. Through the double-glazing they can barely hear a syllable, but they exaggerate the movements of their lips to make it possible to determine what the other is saying. 'Are you here to rescue us, or something?'

Sadly, she shakes her head, unable to make her mouth form the words.

'Then why are you here?'

She holds his gaze. 'I don't even know,' she says. 'I had to come.'

'What is going on? Why have you done this?' His angry breath frosts the glass.

'I haven't done anything,' she protests. 'I was only doing what I was told to do. There was no choice in it.'

'Of course,' Wormwood sneers. 'It's not your fault is it, leaving us to starve in here and rot. Like animals. You were only following orders.'

'But that's the truth,' she says. 'There was no choice. The government gave the orders. There's a virus. It's bad. It's killing a lot of people. The hospitals can't cope. We can't keep everyone alive.'

'You mean the Caveo shareholders gave the orders,' snaps Wormwood. 'You will have noticed that the other lot got out okay.' He gestures violently towards the St Peters section of the complex. 'I guess they crunched their numbers and searched their vacuous little souls and decided it was okay to save the Platinum members and leave the rest of us to fend for ourselves.'

'It's pandemonium out there,' she protests. 'Everything is in lockdown. And where they are now, they are no better off than you, really.'

'You mean they're screwed, too,' he says. 'That's comforting.' Her face betrays the fact that she has no idea if this is more of his dark humour. 'We are not less than them, just less well off. It's hardly the same thing.'

'None of this was easy,' she says. 'You have to believe that.'

Her face is a mask but he can still see her discomfort in her defensive posture, arms crossed stiffly across her chest. He suppresses a smile of bitter satisfaction. 'No, I really don't.'

'I have never lied to you,' she protests. 'It's true I never liked you. Why should I? Who's to say I have to like everyone in my care. It's hard, and I have better things to do than do battle with the likes of you. You are not a likeable man. If that's your way of coping then fine, but don't ask me to like it. You are nothing but a thorn.'

'Thanks for noticing.' He changes his tone. 'So. Are you going to do the Christian thing and let us out of here?'

For the first time, she looks away. 'I can't.'

'Yes, you certainly can. Call it charity.' He notices that her eyes involuntarily look to her hip pocket where she habitually keeps her keys.

'I can't,' she says, 'and I won't. It wouldn't be the right thing to do. Some of you are almost certainly infected so we can't let you out.'

'We?' His face darkens. 'Has His Lordship sent you?'

'No. I came because I had to. By *we*, I mean, the people. The survivors. I shouldn't even be here. Martial law has been declared. There are soldiers everywhere.'

Wormwood bangs on the glass with both hands. 'Open the fucking doors.'

'If it means anything to you, I am genuinely sorry.'

'No,' says Wormwood. 'You are not. You are genuinely feeling sorry for yourself. That thing you are feeling is guilt. I hope it chokes you.'

'You really are a piece of work, Mr Wormwood,' she says.

'Open the doors,' he commands. 'Not for me. For them. I might be scum, as you say, but they deserve better than this. We won't last the week.'

She takes hold of the cross around her neck and puts it to her lips. 'May God have mercy on your souls. Even you, Mr Wormwood.' She turns and walks away. Wormwood stands and watches her diminish into the night that has now swallowed them. Over the intercom system, Bob Marley is informing him that everything is going to be alright, and the thought crosses Wormwood's mind that a few months after that recording reggae's brightest star had also been swallowed by the darkness. He feels old and weak and hungry and he wanders off in search of something to provide a little comfort.

Chapter 8

Amongst the personal possessions that Wormwood chose to bring when he first arrived was a collection of tawdry horror films on DVD, convinced as he was that he would be forced to watch endless reruns of 'Antiques Roadshow' which would be sure to quickly bring on fits of psychosis. Thus was born the notorious weekly battleground between himself and Amanda - inevitably escalating into a fully-fledged conflict with Mr Lord - that became known as Wormwood's Friday Night Film-show. Amongst various zombie titles - again, a little joke at the thought that he too was now joining the ranks of the undead in a care facility for the frail elderly - was a particularly unwholesome little film that proclaimed the sensational tagline: 'The lucky ones died first.' That has now become regrettably apposite for the residents of St Peters. After he has eaten, he calls for a war party and informs James and Windrush what he has just discovered.

'Not like this,' says Windrush. 'No way, man.' He is rarely serious but now his tone is grave. 'There is no way my family is going to leave me to die like this,' he says. It is hard to tell whether this is bravado or a statement of fact.

'What now?' asks James. He has spent the evening tending to others as best he can. Two more residents have slipped way, several are on the brink and it is all he can do to keep their hearts pumping.

Wormwood looks at each of them in turn, 'I honestly don't know,' he says. 'She might even be right. Maybe it's for the best if we just do our duty and curl up and die as quietly as possible. Leave no mess, and all that.'

'Bullshit,' says Windrush. 'If we are infected then so are they.' He is not well educated, but he is widely respected for always speaking common sense. 'If we got it, we got it from them. We're stuck in here. How the hell else are we gonna catch it? First chance we get, we need to be out of here.'

'That's fine for us,' says James. 'But there are only a few of us who could survive long out there. If everything is as Wormwood says, we'll probably be shot. Besides, someone needs to look after the others.'

'There's no food,' says Wormwood, 'and no help is coming.'

'Oh, they're coming alright,' says Windrush. 'Just you wait and see.'

'Okay, that may well be, but no *official* help is coming.' He already suspects that James is dispensing medication to ease people out of their discomfort. He is nicer than the rest of them, a genuinely decent and honest man, but Wormwood has come to know him well enough to know without knowing that he is making painful decisions that are taking their toll. Reluctantly, he has become the boatman over the River Styx. He nods, accepting the cold truth.

Later that evening, an old poet drowns in his bed, calling out for help to let go, finally choking on his words, which is the preferred death of the wordsmith, like the proverbial Roman falling on his sword. James is there by his side, doing what little he can to ease the transition. Rebecca has grown feverish, which is little surprise as the water supply has now been cut off and they have to make do with the water they thought to save in sinks and what few pots they could find. The Peterloo stench has found them in their new home and makes everything twice as hard.

There is no banter anymore. Conversations tend to be whispered and functional, recording the privations and small sufferings as their world turns upside down. Wormwood sits alone, staring out of the window. He has taken to hurling rocks from the garden at the windows in a vain attempt to secure an escape route, but he lacks the strength to make any significant impact. He is aware that this might be it, the final struggle is upon them and he hopes he has the strength to go out well. In the distance, a huge building is ablaze against the horizon. James has come to join him.

'What's that?' he says, struggling to get his bearings.

'The prison,' says Wormwood matter-of-factly.

'Poor bastards,' says James. 'Imagine dying like that.'

Wormwood gives him a stare. 'Right,' he says. 'I can think of worse ways.'

The sight is compelling and he feels shame at being a voyeur. Tiny flames lick at the darkness creating a sort of anti-rainbow of hellish colours across the night sky. He changes the conversation. 'Where's Windrush?'

'He's with Rebecca. She's in a bad way. She hasn't got long left.' The speed with which things are falling apart is quite terrifying. Was it just two days ago that he watched her dance with Windrush a few feet away from where he is now sitting? Can it really be true that what we think of as society is as fragile as a glass paperweight, beautiful and substantial in its own way – until it crashes against a harder reality. From all directions, people are calling out for water, for pity, for divine intervention to release them from their suffering.

Wormwood is overwhelmed. He can hear someone screaming to drown out the noise and is startled to see in the reflected glass that the person is himself. James is at his side. He pushes a moist cloth into his hands.

'This is no time for weakness,' he says. 'Just do what you can.' Wormwood goes to the bedside of someone who is literally gasping for breath. He administers the cloth to the man's forehead to provide what must be a pitifully small degree of comfort. His eyes are beseeching, feebly reaching with the last of his strength for a hand to take his own in his final agonies. It is quite something to wonder what force it is that compels him to fight so hard to cling on what little remains of his life.

'It's okay,' says Wormwood, 'It's okay to let go.' His grip tightens, the careworn eyes look right through him and in an instant he is someplace else beyond suffering. Wormwood has been here before but it has never felt so intimate. His eyes are burning and his limbs are so heavy that it is some time before he eases his fingers from the man's death-grip and rises to his feet. In death, the face has softened, free of suffering and he recognises that this is the grandfather of the boy he has befriended, Jake. He shuffles out of the room, feeling all of his seventy-three years and more. He feels ancient, as if he has risen from clay which has resisted his every effort to free himself. On the horizon, the fire is raging like a portal to hell has opened, threatening to turn night into a false dawn. Everything is crazy. He notices two glowing eyes staring at him. His mind is wandering and he fears it is some kind of unleashed demon. They stare him down, steadily growing larger. With a start, he realises that it is a vehicle of some kind, moving fast, racing round the deserted ring roads that encircle the city and then turning and coming straight at them.

The impact is spectacular as the car smashes through the main atrium. It takes a few seconds for everything to settle as panels of the structure slowly collapse like albino dominoes. Thick fugs of smoke bellow from inside the vehicle and the stink of weed temporarily sweetens the scent of death and decay. A man jumps out. Wormwood recognises him as one of Windrush's family, a grandson.

'Is he alive?' the man calls out. His eyes are wild.

'Through there.' Wormwood gestures nonchalantly in the general direction as if this is an everyday occurrence but the commotion has brought Windrush staggering out. His eyes are rimmed with red, but he lights up when he sees his grandson.

'I knew you'd come,' he calls out.

'You think I was gonna let you die in here?' he says 'Like a slave?' The two men embrace. We've gotta be quick, old man, there's a helicopter out looking for us.'

'What about them?' asks Windrush. He looks over at Wormwood and James.

'Sorry.' The man looks genuinely apologetic but this is no time for sentiment. Sirens can be heard in the distance. 'No room.' With a shrug, he jumps back into the car, turning the key to make sure the engine is still functioning despite the damage it has suffered. 'Come on,' he calls.

The three old men embrace warmly. 'It's fine,' says James. 'We're needed here anyway.'

Wormwood conjures a smile for his old friend. 'You need to get going.' They have to physically manhandle Windrush into the car.

'I will see you again,' he calls out as the car reverses out with some difficulty through the debris, wheel-spins and departs. The headlights are switched off and the night consumes man and boy and car in an instant as the helicopter swooshes overhead in a sweeping pattern searching for lights that have simply disappeared.

James and Wormwood step outside, carefully stepping over debris to avoid injury. It is an instinctive action for those who have been imprisoned, and they share that reticence of prisoners to simply take the first opportunity to escape that has been observed throughout history. It takes a while for the mind to comprehend that the period of captivity may be coming to an end; and then to begin to wonder what freedom might actually mean. The transformative notion of liberty after such a long time seems so enormous that it becomes hard to take the first steps. They stand and watch the helicopter for several minutes before satisfying themselves that it has finally given up hope of tracking the vehicle which has taken their friend into safekeeping. It sweeps away towards the burning prison, presumably looking for escapees. The sky is cloudless, apart from one solitary cloud which has temporarily obscured the supersized moon and thrown a cloak of invisibility over the entire landscape.

'Son of a bitch,' says Wormwood admiringly. 'He did always say that was going to happen.'

'Yes, but did you ever believe it?'

'Not for a single second. I assumed he was doomed, just like the rest of us.'

With the front entrance smashed in, the temperature has fallen dramatically.

'Whatever next.' James wonders out loud. It is not an interrogative but merely a statement of the bewilderment he is feeling, slowly giving way to a numbness which is as much emotional and physical, and partly a result of the cold.

'I can't believe it has happened so fast,' says James. Perhaps this is what happens when the rhythms of your days are institutionalised; anything that happens is magnified out of any sense of perspective. That said, these are extraordinary times. A car has just smashed through the front door in a daring and reckless rescue, after all. 'How has everyone died so quickly?' he wonders. 'Are we really that close to death?' It is a question perhaps best left unasked.

For once, Wormwood has nothing to offer. James suggests that the immediate problem to attend to is to bury the recently deceased.

'I haven't the strength in my bones,' says Wormwood. He is exhausted. Perhaps death is closer than they would like to think. 'In answer to your question, I think all that kept some of them going was the routine. Take that away, and there was nothing else to sustain them.' If true, how sad is that. He comes up with a different idea, one rooted in ancient traditions. 'We have to burn them,' he says. James assumes with some justification that this is to minimise the spread of disease but it is even more practical than that. It requires less effort and they all done in.

Using a metal gurney, they heave the deceased two at a time onto the metal surface and move them to the central garden area where they create a pile of bodies. There is little dignity to the proceedings, but the pain in their aching limbs serves to remind them that even if there was the will to bury them with the respect they deserve, there is no way they could achieve what has become a herculean feat. It takes considerably more than an hour. Wormwood has located some fuel with which to douse the bodies. His face is a frozen mask, expressionless, whilst James stands to one side, nauseated by the ghastly spectacle. Wormwood struggles to light a match, his fingers shaking with exhaustion and cold rather than emotion. His friend has become used to Wormwood's unpredictability, but even he is shocked at what follows. Wormwood takes a piece of smouldering wood at then uses it to light the curtains inside St Peters. They catch light quickly, and a light blaze soon pushes the flames to other parts of the complex.

'What the hell have you done?' James screams at him, not with anger but because the crackling flames are almost deafening as they really start to catch hold.

'What needed to be done. To hell with all of it.' Wormwood has taken the few remaining residents and pushed their beds outside through the debris that used to central as the main entrance. They are covered with blankets, and he has calculated that they are at a safe distance from the flammable parts of the complex and that the fire will keep them warm enough to last until the first rays of morning sun.

'There is no more food anyway,' he points out. 'If people see the blaze and care enough to come, they will be safe. If not, they were already dead.' James is hardly surprised at Wormwood's pragmatism and seeming indifference to suffering. What little he has revealed about his time in the armed forces has been sufficient to reveal that Wormwood is well trained to make cold and calculated decisions in the most dire of circumstances.

Fantastically dressed in a floral duvet slung around his shoulders to keep out the cold, Wormwood trudges into the darkness. His way is illuminated by the moon which has now emerged from obscurity, and the inconsistent brilliance of the raging fire. He looks once over his shoulder. 'You coming?' he asks.

'Sure,' says James, stumbling over debris and slipping on spilled engine oil as he struggles to keep up. 'Why ever not?' He knows better than to ask such a foolish question as to whether Wormwood has any idea where they are heading. Of course he doesn't, other than to find themselves somewhere else, somewhere safe, by day's break. Beneath their feet, Wormwood can feel something ancient stirring, the dull sounds of metal weapons being readied for a future battle. Although technically they are making their way quietly thought the night, their stories are far from done.

In the time-honoured tradition of all escapees, they let blind luck and raw instinct guide their way, although Wormwood has a decent understanding of the local geography and leads the way. They are ill-equipped to be out is such conditions, but the dying vapours of adrenaline give them the strength they require to find a place to rest. Orion looms above them in the night sky; aged, exhausted, they are the Hunter's aching shoulders, Bellatrix and Betelgeuse.

It transpires that Wormwood's local knowledge is out of date, like an atlas from a previous era, but with good fortune on his side they stumble across a coffee shop franchise on a service road to an A road to somewhere. It has been secured with wooden boards, but clearly by college students who have never before wielded a hammer. With ease, the men pry loose a couple of boards, force a window and gain entry, reaching back on themselves to pull the boards to. There are uneaten sandwiches in a refrigerated unit and they eat their fill, though most combinations of ingredients are so alien to them that it is hard to call it a pleasant experience. At least their hunger is sated. Miraculously, the heating works, too. It is truly a night of wonders; the horrors, hopefully, have been left far behind.

Conversation has been largely functional throughout the long walk. Now that some comfort has been secured, words begin to flow a little more freely. Wormwood has become feverish with the desire for vengeance, though he is reduced to mumbling vague incoherent threats to nameless people who will suffer when he becomes reacquainted with real time. He feels dislocated, disjointed, disheartened.

'The bastards know who they are,' he cries out. 'They know the day of judgement is at hand.' But his voice is feeble, the petulant raging of a victim who knows neither the names or the faces of those who have sinned against him. James gives voice to his parental concerns regarding his daughter. Age and infirmity have not diminished that atavistic protective role that nature endowed when he first held his child.

'I can't help but worry,' he says. 'She's all I have left.'

'Of course,' Wormwood agrees. 'Priority number one. But for the moment there's nothing we can do.' They each select a place where they can lie down and hope that sleep will soon overtake them. Wormwood is still raging inside his head. His synapses are furiously mis-firing and he suffers what is probably a minor stroke, his mind wandering as he himself has wandered this night, seeing himself as the head of a fierce army of warriors brandishing well-used weapons as they march towards an unknown enemy. At various times, he cries out in his sleep, though there is not a force on earth or beyond that is capable of waking James.

They wake almost at the same time late in the morning, the wooden boards having done a fine job of shutting out the light. Their limbs ache, but the extended rest has rejuvenated them somewhat. Wormwood is groggy, as you might expect, but he is revived by the coffee that his friend prepares for him. Reluctantly, they eat more food that seems like something you might encounter on a trip overseas, such is the random combination of tastes and textures that assaults their mouths.

'Who on earth would choose to eat this crap?' Wormwood grumbles, but it does what even bad food manages to do, which it is to fill the void in his stomach. There is a newspaper in a waste-bin which contains some information about the virus, though it is a week old. The information is sketchy as various so-called experts in their field attempt to make a name for themselves by advocating a theory to explain what has so stricken the country and, so it would appear, the world at large. It is soon clear that no one has a clue what has happened, except that this plague is a true socialist, afflicting rich and poor, young and old, black and white, with equal vigour. They are more interested to read about the passing of an emergency act of parliament, the Civil Obedience Act, which has introduced draconian measures to keep the spread of virus to a minimum. All non-essential services have been curtailed. An early evening curfew is in place with heavy penalties for non-compliance. In an attempt to curb misinformation leading to the spread of the virus through ignorance or even acts of civil non-compliance, which radicals and some liberals will resort to when martial law is declared, all broadcast and social media has been suspended. There is a thirty minute government broadcast on the BBC every evening at 6, with public information films regarding the symptoms, medical treatment and ways of avoiding exposure broadcast every fifteen minutes on repeat.

James is single-minded in his response. 'How on earth am I going to make sure Sally is okay?'

'You know the answer,' says Wormwood. 'There is only one way. We have to go to see her for ourselves.'

There is a map of the area posted on a wall in the coffee outlet, as if there is any great demand for tourist information. They quickly calculate that she lives about three miles away, a distance which manages to be both reassuringly close but frustratingly far enough away to pose a physical challenge.

'I just need to know,' says James, to which his friend nods in agreement.

'We need to wait until the light is failing. That way, we've less chance of getting picked up on the way.'

Until that point, they haven't really thought through the implications of their abandonment at the hands of the authorities. If it is, as they suspect, some cynical piece of Malthusian policy-making which has determined that resources are better spent on the young and fit then they can expect a hostile reaction if they are picked up on the run, breaking curfew and who knows how many other Kafkaesque rules governing civil obedience. James is so single-minded that has not even thought to ask if his friend has any plans of his own. Wormwood has never openly spoken about family, and certainly never received a visit in his eighteen months or so in Peterloo, but no-one missed the look on his face when Amanda once taunted him about the fact that he had no family visits again after a particularly spiteful period of enmity between the two arch-foes.

They spend the afternoon planning a route. For the main part, Wormwood employs his military training to get them most of the way to the target without being intercepted, though at one point an exasperated James is compelled to point out that they are not fighting bloody Zulus.

'Overkill on the details?' he asks.

'Just a tad.' James knows the estate on which his daughter lives pretty well, including a secluded pathway well used by dog-walkers which would certainly offer the best chance of protection and cover. Between them, a plan of action is agreed.

And then it starts to rain, not the thin drizzle that habitually falls in these parts but something akin to a storm. In terms of providing additional cover, it is not the worst thing to happen, but it affords a level of discomfort which brings little joy to the prospect of an overland hike. They rummage through cupboards and find bin bags with which they fashion crude raincoats by pulling holes for heads and arms. Looking at each other, they resemble crazed old men escaped from an asylum, almost enough to crack a smile. James is not sure he doesn't prefer this Wormwood better than the malcontent who killed time picking pointless fights and scoring pyrrhic victories in a communal day-room which now seems like something that happened in their past, not mere days ago. This Wormwood has more purpose, and is able to draw meaningfully on all those past experiences which have shaped him, those emotional and physical impacts which have scarred him inside and out like heavenly bodies crashing into the moon.

They set off. Like elementals, they curse through mud and sludge across fields and over fences, preferring to stay away from roads whenever the sweep of headlights sprays across the flattened landscape, though they see only two vehicles in the hour or so it takes them to make headway. Once James has got his bearings, he takes the lead, taking them through forested paths where they encounter startled deer. An owl hoots mournfully for them, two ghosts who have miserably gone in search of the living.

Rounding a corner, they almost literally stumble across a muntjac deer on the path in front of them. They freeze, not wishing to distress the startled animal. Its fur looks russet under the moon's harsh glare, its eyes pools of liquid darkness.

'What on earth is it?' hisses James in a barely audible whisper. 'It's a weird little thing.'

'It's a deer. A muntjac. They're Chinese.'

The shock of seeing a living thing unexpectedly has thrown James a little. 'What's it doing here?' he asks.

'Same as us,' says Wormwood. 'Just trying to survive.' The deer gives them one last lingering look and then disappears noiselessly into the undergrowth.

'Bloody hell,' says James, breathing out as if he has been holding his breath throughout the whole encounter. 'What's a Chinese deer doing out here, eh?'

Wormwood sighs, too, but for different reasons. 'They escaped from a zoo when they pulled down the iron railings during the war for munitions.'

'Escapee, eh?' says James. 'Just like us, then. Scared the living Jesus out of me, but I guess I can forgive it.' He smiles weakly at his friend. His breathing slowly returns to normal and they move on.

Finally, they near houses. Over fences, they can see the spectral glow of television sets illuminating rooms. A silhouette of a woman can be seen in an upstairs window, causing James to look away in embarrassment. Across the way, two kids are getting high in breach of curfew in the hinterland between garden and treeline. His feet wet, James is not happy, but this is largely because proximity to his daughter has amplified his anxiety. He signals them to pause to make sure they have not been seen, but the kids are too far gone to notice or care. It is all they can to stand up, leaning against trunks to support their weight as they float into space inside themselves.

James beckons them on. There is a small overgrown path that leads closer to the houses and then they push through a hedge and find themselves in a suburban back garden. A security light catches movement and they are illuminated like burglars. James freezes, but Wormwood has taken him in hand and instinctively pulls him over to one side where the light cannot penetrate. Breathless, they wait. After a short while, an interior light turns on and a male figure is back-lit in a doorway.

'I've called the police,' a voice calls out. 'Whoever you are, you'd better fuck off right now.' The exterior lights flicker off.

James rolls his eyes. He mouths the words *son-in-law* and gestures rudely with his hand. Wormwood smiles at that. The rain has finally eased off but they are literally soaked through and it takes some effort for James to push through foliage to stand on the back lawn. He is aware that he must look like some mythic beast in the dark, something parents might use to terrify children into obedience.

'I'm armed,' the voice calls out.

'No, you're not, you big dickhead,' says James wearily. 'It's me. James.' The security lights punctuate the moment perfectly by switching back on.

'Oh, for fuck's sake,' says the son-in-law, breathing heavily with relief. His name is Barry and it suits him. 'What the fuck are you doing here?'

James is exasperated. 'What do you think I'm doing?' There is a tone of voice he only uses on his son-in-law. 'I'm worried about Sally. I needed to make sure she's okay.'

'You can't be here,' says Barry. 'You must have heard. There's a curfew. Everyone is in lockdown.' His voice is growing louder with anger, then he realises the neighbours might hear and he switches to a villainous hiss.

'You might even be infectious. You're the very last thing we need right now.'

James is taken aback by his animosity. 'Can I just see her?' he asks.

'James, you need to fuck off. Right now.'

Wormwood has had enough. He now stands at his friend's side. 'Go and fetch his daughter,' he commands.

Like most bullies, Barry's aggressiveness is a sort of bubble that encircles him, easily blown away. He stands his ground long enough to make a crude point and then he disappears inside. There is an angry exchange. When he comes back a minute or so later, he has his wife in front of him like a shield, though he holds on to her with both hands.

She is holding back tears. 'Dad!' she cries out. 'What are you doing here?'

He is shaking. 'Are you okay?' he asks. 'And George and Daisy? I had to know.'

'Dad, I'm fine. We're all fine. But what are you doing here? This virus, it's so awful. It's been a nightmare.' She tries to pull away, to run to her father, but Barry, standing behind her, has a fast grip on her shoulders.

'Are you both crazy?' he hisses. 'Are you trying to get us all infected?' In the distance, a siren can be heard, growing louder with each breath as she strains against him.

'I'm so sorry,' she calls out. 'Look after yourself, dad. It will all be over soon.'

As husband grapples wife back into the house, so Wormwood pulls his friend back into the darkness. Reluctantly, they retrace their steps back through the treeline and withdraw into heavy foliage which resists the beams of torches that criss-cross the area. As they wait for the police to give in, they each hear the echo of Sally's last words.

It will all be over soon.

Contenting themselves with the capture of the kids hiding not thirty feet away, the police soon depart. The old men can hear the police manhandling the youths, shouting at them for endangering others and taking the opportunity to vent their own lingering fears of infection. Civil liberties are the first casualties of a mass panic, it would appear.

They rest awhile. 'You weren't kidding,' says Wormwood. 'He really is a piece of work.'

'I did tell you,' says James. 'I honestly don't what we did wrong. What she sees in him I just don't know.'

'Do you want to go back and get her?' asks Wormwood, evidently not joking.

The prolonged silence tells him that James is considering it, weighing up options. He shakes his head. 'For now at least, she's safer where she is. I mean, what can we offer her?'

It is a good point. The rain has now stopped but clouds conspire to obscure the moon and cover their tracks as they begin the long trudge back to relative safety, warmth and shelter. There are no words, but both men are thinking much the same thing, which is how much worse could things get and how much longer are they able to keep going. And all the time there is that ear-worm, burrowing deeper into their ravaged brains:

It will all be over soon.

Chapter 9

If you are well read, you will appreciate that even the boldest revolutionaries and *great men* of history, good and bad, have prolonged periods of inaction, as if they are merely waiting for time to catch up with them. Even Jesus must have spent much of his youth apprenticed as a carpenter before the crowds started to gather and the miracles began to attract attention. Hitler lived in flophouses in obscurity and poverty, whilst Che Guevara roamed around a continent on a bike, healing lepers, playing football and screwing women.

Two days pass whilst Wormwood ponders his next move. His entire life he has felt himself thwarted. He feels the essence of himself fading with each passing day, in terms of the time it takes him to come to in the morning and recover from his exertions, although counter-intuitively he feels sharper than he has in quite some time when he is finally awake. James largely leaves him to it, taking on the challenge of cleaning and drying their things as a way to distract himself from his other concerns over which he has little, if any, control. Instinctively, he senses that his friend is plotting, devising schemes, running through the potential outcomes of each course of action. That brooding face is an inscrutable mask, hypothesising and calculating, though with each period of contemplation he concludes with a snort, a fresh coffee, and more prolonged silence. It hardly helps that his mind is wandering, like a trolley with a lame wheel, steering him on tangential tracks of thought that lead down blind alleys and ultimately, nowhere.

'Stupid old fool.' He curses himself for all his old failings, relying too much on the power of his intellect to guide him through difficult times, always believing the old lie that there is a good deed or wise words which will lead to a positive outcome.

He rejoins James, who has fallen back on the old habit of watching wasps smash their heads against glass, attracted no doubt by the sugar or syrups which he uses to sweeten the beverage that passes for coffee. Distractedly, he watches the wasp bounce over and again into the glass, temporarily stunned and then more determined than ever. His own face is reflected in the glass with the boards behind it holding his reflection. Frustration suits him, his brooding visage scowling back at him. He actually looks fresher, more vital, than he has for some time, despite the indignity of toileting in a public washroom. The effort of thought, genuine contemplation, rather than the ill-natured trouble-making that had marked his time at St Peters, has enervated him. His mind wanders. Objectively, he observes his disembodied self watching the futile droning fury of the wasp caught behind glass, and he sees himself with a clarity that has hitherto eluded him. With horror, like a patsy who realises he has been duped into carrying a suicide vest, he recognises that he is the wasp. It is a damascene moment, and he slumps into a wipe-down chair to allow the enormity of his self-realisation to wash over him.

He is the wasp.

Blinded by a single-mindedness – or simple-mindedness – to smash through obstacles at great personal and physical cost rather than trying to see a way around it. There is a vent in the window which has been cracked for ventilation purposes, but the wasp is unable to follow the breeze and escape. The ledge below is littered with the dried husks of other insects and yet the wasp furiously buzzes away into the glass again and again and again in an almost hypnotic rhythm.

The rest of the evening, the idea slowly crystallises in his mind. Perhaps because he is in such a diminished state, it never even occurs to him that perhaps his synapses are making faulty electrical connections, seeing things that don't actually exist. Finally, he thinks he can see a way forward and the thought of it is soothing to his troubled mind.

The first step is to recover their strength. In a weakened state, anything they do is likely to fail. James has brought some medication with him from Peterloo and informs him that they are well stocked with the essentials for the immediate future. With the refrigerator stuffed with out-of-date but edible food and drink, they are not likely to starve. Wormwood tells him that they need to be strategic in their thinking. Whatever they do next should be purposeful. They have to assume that they it will be presumed they have perished in the fire at St Peters, unless Barry has contacted the police, which they decide he is unlikely to have done.

'At the moment, it's hard to see what needs to be done,' says Wormwood, thinking out loud. 'We can't predict how things are going to develop, so we need to be patient. We have to stop raging around like old fools with brains full of holes.'

'Speak for yourself,' says James, but he knows there is much truth in it.

It is clear that neither one of them has given up the fight, yet, unlike many of their former co-residents in St Peters who had ceased to be vital almost as soon as their routine was broken. The rapidity of their deterioration was as shocking as it was instructive.

'We have make sure that we remain functional. Things won't go on like this forever so we just need to sit things out and see how the land lies when we move into the next phase. I know that your main priority is your daughter and your grandchildren, so we also need to make sure that they all come out of this okay.'

'Thanks,' says James. 'You know that means a lot. What about you?'

Wormwood pulls one of those faces that foretell nothing but trouble. 'Someone has to pay for all of this. I don't know who they are yet, but people have made decisions and I have lost people I care about. I am sad and I am angry and I know that I have to do something about it. I need to channel all this rage into something positive, something to lead me out of the darkness.'

In the morning, they risk going outside. There are moulded plastic benches crafted to resemble wood for people who prefer to drink their coffees outside. The rain has freshened things up and a weak sun warms them a little. They can see for miles across a reclaimed landscape flattened by gravity. The spires of a cathedral and the bland oblong of a shopping centre lend some substance to the horizon. To their left, the husk of the prison still exhales wisps of smoke into the sky. Though widely derided for the bland monotony of its flora, both men have come to see some beauty in this land which has been rescued from the sea, the former tidal marshes and floodplains secretly nurturing plants whose roots anchor the modest history of the place. Ancient kings have fought sea-faring invaders here. Warrior queens have done battle with Romans and their shed blood has nurtured the earth which is now the best farmland in the country. Some beauty may never find itself replicated on a biscuit tin, but that doesn't mean it doesn't exist. It is question not of looking but seeing.

They each cradle a craft coffee which have grown not to dislike, probably brewed from beans recovered from the excrement of Asian mammals, or whatever. The following night, they decide, they will go back and try to isolate Sally to speak to her without the bullying presence of her husband, who will undoubtedly be watchful for their return. It is not clear how they will achieve this, but they are both confident that it can be done, and that it will be helpful to learn more about the current state of play with the virus and the response of the authorities to the ongoing threat.

'If we are infectious, we need to know,' says James. 'The last thing I want to do is harm my family.' With that in mind, they decide to wait a few more days to return to the house. To pass the time, they entertain each other with different scenarios in which they assault Barry with various garden implements borrowed from the shed. James shreds his face with a hypothetical rake, whereas Wormwood prefers the flat of a spade to bludgeon him into bloody submission.

Close proximity for prolonged periods of time breeds either contempt or a special kind of intimacy reserved for a true confidante.

'Is there actually something wrong with you?' asks James when their imagination has run its course. 'I never used to be like this, you know.'

'Don't delude yourself,' says Wormwood. 'I knew as soon as I met you that you couldn't possibly be as nice as you seemed to be.' He stresses the word *nice* as if it is a curse. 'I knew there was darkness in you. Same as the rest of us. You just needed the right circumstances to let it out.'

'And what was that?'

'Your family, obviously,' says Wormwood. 'What wouldn't you be capable of in order to protect them?' They move into the kitchen, selecting different utensils as weapons to continue their imaginary attack. When they get to the whisk, they realise that the joke has probably runs its course.

'This suits you, you know,' says James.

'What? Being on the run?' He cracks a smile. 'Not the first time I've heard that.'

'Not just that,' says James. 'All of it. You just seem more...alive somehow.'

Wormwood turns his head to face his friend. His face suddenly seems sad. 'In answer to your previous question, I think that there are undoubtedly a lot of people would agree that there is something very wrong with me. They've probably formed some kind of private club to discuss their own personal grievances against me.'

'Oh, who cares what Amanda thinks,' says James. 'You did go way too far with winding her up sometimes, but she was a complete witch. Dreadful woman. Or Lord, for that matter. He was no better.'

Wormwood breathes a deep sigh of something enigmatic and slowly exhales. 'It runs a bit deeper than that, my friend.' He is silent for a time, lost in recollection of darker times. 'I've had it worse than this,' he says. 'Far worse. I've done harder time in my past lives than being stuck in a crummy care home with staff who - mostly - don't give a damn about you.' The passing reference to the one exception to the rule, the deep-clean lady, takes both of them to a happier place in their heads.

'I was in prison for a while,' he says, his voice flattening. 'That wasn't great.'

'We had suspected as much,' says James. 'Not because of the way you were, but some of the things His Lordship insinuated when you had pushed hard at him.'

'Yeah, he was fond of bringing that up on our regular private sessions. He made it quite clear that he was doing me some kind of huge favour accommodating a *bad seed* such as myself. He was such a sanctimonious prick.'

'Bad seed,' James chuckled. He likes that description, storing it in his ravaged memory bank for future use.

'Aren't you going to ask me what I was inside for?'

James looks away. He is dying to know. 'I'm sure that if you wanted me to know you would already have told me. It's your business.'

Wormwood clenches his fists. His face is conflicted. He is not ashamed of his past, but there are memories he would rather let fall through the holes in his head. 'Short fuse,' he says. 'Poor impulse control. I beat a man who asked for it but he was badly hurt and I got sent down for it. I suspect I didn't make a compelling case for myself with the jury. The other guy was in a coma for a while, and to be honest I was struggling to show much sympathy.'

He waits for James to press for more detail. Like a puzzle, he tells the tale in fragments, like shards of glass in a broken picture frame. He caught him in bed with his wife. There was a confrontation. Blows were exchanged. The other man ends up in a coma and, apparently, his kids liked him more.

'So that was that. I got 18 months. Ended up serving nearly seven years. Turns out I had a big mouth and kept talking myself into trouble.'

'Go figure.' James whistles in mock shock. 'I can't imagine you digging a hole for yourself like that at all.'

Wormwood laughs. 'Kept digging until I nearly dug my own grave. I guess it was like a slow suicide. It's amazing I ever got out at all.'

He decides they need another coffee. They have progressed to coffee with syrup, more for variety than for the taste of it. Wormwood pours it like a cocktail waiter, distracting himself momentarily from unpleasant remembrances of time past.

'The sad joke of it, I've spent most of my life in one prison or another. My childhood. The army. Marriage. Prison, literally, then Peterloo and now this.' Raising a glass, he toasts the coffee franchise which he now calls home. 'In fact, this is about as good as it's ever been.'

James is reeling from one revelation after another, but he lets his friend keep talking. Sometimes, the wisest course of action is just to shut up and listen, the irony of which is that this is a truism that his friend has evidently never learned.

Chapter 10

There is quite a commotion going on, pushing and scuffling noises signifying a physical confrontation.

'Why don't you just shut the hell and listen, you dumb bitch!'

Barry has his wife gripped by the throat against a wall, his anger fuelled by her unwillingness to submit. She is not of the generation who will simply accept abuse as an inevitable fact of life; she is programmed to resist as best she can. However, her hands are tied by that need to protect her children which is encoded in her DNA. She pulls fingers loose and struggles to find the air to form words. 'Not in front of the kids.'

'Fuck them,' he snarls. 'Let them see. If you really cared about them, you wouldn't risk all of our lives.' He releases her and her own hands instinctively go to her throat, gasping for breath. She sees her children on the stars, staring in mute horror at her through the bannister, like bars in a prison cell. Her eyes are pleading at them to stop watching. Barry slams the door.

'I don't understand why you're being like this,' she says, her hands still defensively at her throat. 'The world is going to shit all around us. How is any of this my fault?'

He stalks up and down the room, clenching and unclenching his fists. 'How are we supposed to live if you don't have a job? Have you even thought of that?'

She stands up to him, faces him. 'It is not my fault that I lost my job. You can't have it both ways, you bastard. If you won't let me out of the house, how can I go to work?'

'Tell them you'll work from home. Call them back. Do it now.'

He hands her the phone and she tosses it angrily aside. 'There's no use,' she says. 'I work in a supermarket. How the hell can I work from home?'

'Don't talk to me like I'm some kind of idiot,' he snaps.

'Then don't be one. They just told me my contract had been terminated and that was that. No negotiation. No compensation. It's over.'

'Call them back.' He is, as he ever was, a simplistic one-trick pony.

'And say what? Please can I have my job back? Because my useless feckless husband is incapable of holding down a job so he has to parasite off me.' She glares at him. She sees violence fermenting in his eyes. He has never raised a hand to her, but abuse has many faces, each one uniquely insidious.

It is his turn to be defensive. 'You know why I can't work.' Instinctively, he goes through the pantomime of feeling his bad back. 'That's typical of you to bring up something like that.' There is a stand-off. They each feel that they are standing on the edge of a precipice, close to saying words that can never be unspoken. Those dark truths that couples share that are capable of summoning demons of one sort or another.

There is a ping at the window. Then another.

'What the hell.' Barry is relieved for the distraction. He goes to the window and peers out over the garden. He puts his face to the glass as a larger missile bounces off, causing a chip to appear. Furious, he is off towards the back door, flying out into the garden. Sally stands at the door, peering out into the gloom. Indistinct shapes are grappling on the grass.

'Get off me, you idiot.' It is her father's voice, struggling for breath just as hers had been a few moments before. Then there is a sickening metallic thudding noise and a groan and she sees a second man holding a spade like some kind of spectral samurai. Barry comes staggering back into the house and tries to push the door to, but he is holding his head with one hand and is clumsy and imprecise in his actions. Blood is running through his fingers. The man with the spade enters the kitchen, brandishing it as if looking for the excuse to deliver a telling blow. Instinctively, she helps her husband to a wooden chair and allows the man to enter, her father following with him.

'Keep back!' Barry holds up a bloodied hand to keep them at bay. 'The virus, remember.'

They keep their distance. James' hands are working at his throat, trying to get the blood flowing. 'You okay?' he asks.

'No,' says Barry. 'I'm bloody not.'

'Not you, you daft bastard!'

'I'm okay,' says Sally. 'Honest, I'm fine.' She has finger-shaped welts rising across her throat.

Wormwood is still holding the spade menacingly. 'I told you this was the garden weapon of choice,' he says happily.

James grins. 'Looks like we arrived at just the right time,' he says. 'If he ever tries to lay hands on you again, I swear I will kill him.'

'You and whose army?' says Barry, emboldened by his small victory wrestling an old man to the ground. He is still the playground bully, employing the same petty taunts.

Wormwood cracks him another sharp blow to the top of the head. 'This army. Keep talking like that and I'll be burying you in the garden by night's end.' And he pulls a face that lets anyone know that it wouldn't be the first time. Not the first time this week, in fact, as we are well aware.

Sally wets a towel and hands it to her husband who applies it tenderly to his crown with his red right hand. It is hard for her not to run and throw her arms around her father's neck. 'Are you okay?' she asks from a safe distance.

'Oh, you don't need to worry about us,' says James. 'Things didn't work out as St Peters but we've found a new place. It's much better.' He becomes aware that his voice sounds less than convincing.

'We're doing just fine,' says Wormwood. 'The new place gives us a lot more freedom.' He gestures with the spade towards the pathetic man at the table with his head in his hands. 'What about him?' It is an open question to the room. James meets his daughter's eyes, communicating without words.

'We can easily make him go away,' says Wormwood helpfully.

'What? Kill him?' James protests. 'He's still father to my grandkids.'

Wormwood laughs out loud. 'Bloody hell,' he booms. 'What do you take me for? I only meant we could take his keys and kick him out. We can hardly leave him here, can we. I know you. You wouldn't sleep for worry.'

They know he is right. A line has been crossed. Sally says nothing, lets the responsibility for it fall on others for once. She finds his keys in his jacket pocket and tosses them on the table. His voice is what can only be described as snivelling, not pathetic, for that implies pity and there is precious little of that in the room for him. 'Where am I supposed to go?' he protests.

'Not our problem,' says James. He hauls his son-in-law to his feet and pushes him towards the front door, which his wife obligingly holds open for him. Two faces have appeared at the top of the stairs, their faces streaked with tears.

'Daisy,' he cries out. 'George, aren't you going to help me?' His damning answer is the silence, apart from the brave snuffling of suppressed tears. Unceremoniously, he is pushed outside and the door locked to him. Through the front window, Sally stands and watches him stand there, suddenly quite small and vulnerable in the enormity of the uncertain world that awaits. Towel still pressed to his head, his face marred by blood, he finally gives up and walks away.

James has made a round of drinks, taking the opportunity to check fridge and cupboards to ensure there is a decent store of provisions. They drink in silence around the table, the chairs arranged at a safe distance. The children have joined them for hot chocolate, but they are careful not to get too close.

'Who are you?' asks the girl with that bluntness that only children can get away with.

'Never mind me,' says Wormwood. 'I'm just some old man.'

'You look sad,' she says. James takes a close look at him. She is right. His face wears that haunted look that betrays a heavy dose of déjà vu. He is travelling in time again and the strain of it is plain to see, simultaneously in the room but also in a very different room in another decade, where he is the man being forced to walk away from his family. It is a science fiction cliché that time does not travel in straight lines, that it is cyclical, a spiral, like strands of DNA.

How is it possible to be both the aggressor and the victim, over and over again?

'I'm fine,' he says, snapping out of it. He smiles, a warm smile that James has never seen before, a smile that comes from a different age when his friend was able to be a very different kind of man.

'Is he coming back?' asks the boy. He is older, and uses a tone that signifies he has been forced to be older than his tender years. There is nothing about the question that suggests he wants the answer to be affirmative, and nobody feels the need to provide him with an answer. He reaches for his mother's hand and she accepts it, glad for the human contact.

'You need to go, too,' says Sally, addressing her father. 'You know how spiteful he can be, especially when he's feeling sorry for himself.'

'Which is all the time,' says the boy.

'You're right,' says James. 'I was planning to stay here to make sure you're safe. But of course, the first thing he'll do is call the police.'

'Are you in trouble, grandad?' asks the girl. She is still innocent enough to see the world in simple binaries of right and wrong, good and bad.

'Of course not,' he says warmly. 'But I have to go back to where I live. Remember? It's not safe for us to be here in case we infect you.'

The girl accepts that. 'Stay safe,' she says. She has learned the words off by heart already.

'You too,' he says. He turns to his daughter and produces a smile. 'I didn't mean for any of this to happen. You'll be okay?'

'Of course,' she says, though her voice is sad. 'It was bound to happen sooner or later. Please take care of him,' she says to Wormwood.

'Of course.'

Like sinners slipping away, they exit through the back door and take the well-trodden path back from whence they came. Brambles catch at their clothes and pull threads that will wear into holes if they live long enough.

'Will she be okay?' asks Wormwood. 'She seems quite capable.'

'She is,' says James. He is breathing a little hard to keep up with his friend, though his slowness of step is as much born of his reluctance to leave. 'She had to be. Her mum died when she was only twelve. She had to grow up fast. She's more resilient than she seems.'

'Good.' He stops to get his bearings and allow himself time to catch his breath. Any traces of adrenaline have long since dissipated and he is starting to feel that sudden crash. 'We can come back in a few days. Check up on them. Make sure they have everything they need.'

'Thanks,' says James.

'Can I ask you something?' asks Wormwood. 'You're a lovely guy. It would have been easy for you to find someone else to marry. I know it must have been hard, and you had Sally to think about, but you must have thought about it.'

James is silent for a while, allowing the question to roll around his head 'To be honest, I never really thought about it. I was just so happy when we were together that it would have seemed dishonest to start again with someone else.' The night has cooled a little but the air is refreshing and the walk is less arduous than on previous journeys, despite the occasional need for a rest. 'I'm sure she wouldn't have minded, and Sally has always just wanted me to be happy, but I just didn't feel like I needed it. As awful as it was losing her, I knew how lucky I had been to get the years we had together. Does that make sense?'

They have arrived back at the coffee franchise and Wormwood is straining to heave the board loose enough for them to clamber back inside. 'It does,' he says. 'I can't say I particularly enjoyed the whole marriage thing, but I don't regret it either. I just wish it had turned out better.'

'Never thought about settling down again?'

Wormwood snorts. 'In prison? Not really my thing.' They struggle through the window and out of habit get a brew going. They aren't going to sleep any time soon.

'What about after?'

'After?' Wormwood considers that for a moment. 'I wouldn't have inflicted myself on someone I cared about after that,' he says.

'You inflicted yourself on us,' says James, trying to lighten the mood a little.

'That's different. Look at the trouble you get me into all the time. Fighting in people's kitchens.' He waves a finger reproachfully. 'You are such a bad influence.'

'No-one asked you to smash him over the head with a spade,' says James, his face brightening with laughter.

'Better than using a rake.' They return to that debate again as a happy alternative to reminiscing about lost love, and then spend a mostly sleepless night trying to remind themselves that drinking a stimulant late at night is not conducive to a good night's sleep. Foolish old men, drifting through dreams that haunt one and console another.

Chapter 11

Two nights later they are rudely awakened by the sound of people breaking in. Using a barista's apron to muffle the sound, Wormwood smashes an emptied beer bottle to fashion a crude weapon as two indistinct shapes tumble into the main room through the front door.

There is some confusion as the two parties confront each other at a distance once they each become aware of the other's presence. It turns out to be two Polish men who have been stealthily making their way eastwards towards the coast, hoping to find or steal a boat to get to the mainland. They have not eaten for at least two days so James prepares some food for them while they give an account of what life is like for those breaking curfew.

'We have been chased halfway across the country,' says one of the men. 'It's ridiculous. We've both had the virus. I'm fine. He's fine. We're not carriers. It's crazy out there. I swear there was a wild animal stalking us a little while back.'

'We just want to get home,' says the other. From his pocket, he produces a medical note confirming that he is not infectious. They are builders, and there is little prospect of any building work taking place for the foreseeable future, hence the decision to go home. They recount stories of being pursued by helicopters, threatened by armed police, the stuff of movie nightmares.

'We can't wait to be out of here.' They have no idea whether things are as crazy on the continental mainland, but they agree that it can't be much worse, so once they have eaten, they pack some food and are on their way again.

Despite the warnings, they risk sitting outside later in the afternoon with fresh brews. The sky is huge, a vast canvas which overwhelms the landscape and reduces them to insignificant specks. Their most pressing concern is a shortage of clothing. They have made use of a small supply of lost property dumped in a cupboard, and James has made a crude attempt at washing their clothes, so currently they are sitting outside in nothing but vest and pants.

About a mile to their right is the start of some woodland and a creature appears at its edge. At first they assume it is a dog of some kind, or an oversized fox, but its movements are not right. It has a sleek feline flow which indicates that it is some form of big cat. It stops and sniffs the air. Perhaps it has caught their scent. They are unalarmed, entranced, the distance between them more than sufficient for them to take shelter should it decide to approach. Instinctively, they drink more cautiously, placing their mugs down with greater care lest it make a noise. A brisk wind refreshes them, though their regimen of self-care is generally pretty good for people deemed incapable of such routines not three weeks previously. Their absence of clothes makes both men feel strangely vulnerable. The cat moves on, pauses, springs forward and takes a rabbit in its jaws.

'I've read about this,' says James in a whisper. 'They call it the fen tiger. People assumed it was just a hoax to attract tourists. I guess they were wrong all along.'

'I'm not Attenborough,' says Wormwood, 'but that is no tiger.'

'No stripes. It's big, though,' James insists. 'It's definitely something. Is there a zoo around here?'

'There are zoos everywhere,' says Wormwood. 'You know how we humans love to put things in cages.' They watch it for a few more minutes and then it disappears into the treeline.

'Do you know about the fen tigers?' asks Wormwood.

James feigns confusion. 'Of course, he says. 'We've just seen one of them.' He finishes his drink. 'They were locals, weren't they, opposed to the draining of the fens. They went round sabotaging things and attacking drainage workers brought in from outside.'

'For generations they had happily lived off the land, fishing and catching wildfowl. Then the rich decided the land was theirs and they just took it for themselves. A whole way of life just wiped out, just like that.' Wormwood snaps his fingers. 'They brought the Dutch in to build dykes and earthworks, just so they could create farmland and get even richer. The fenfolk did what they could to stop it.'

'And failed, 'says James. 'As it always is, nothing gets in the way of profit. Progress, I mean.'

'At least they put up some resistance,' says Wormwood. 'Here we are, two old fools still talking about them, centuries later.'

'So, what you're saying,' says James with amusement, 'is that you would most certainly have been a fen tiger.'

'Would have been?' says Wormwood. 'I am a fen tiger. Let my enemies beware.' He brandishes an imaginary weapon over his head, a spade perhaps, and lets out a roar.

'You know this area well,' says James.

'Born and raised,' says Wormwood. 'It's in my blood and my bones. This is brick country, dating back even to the Romans. The dust gets into everything. When I was just a kid, this was my stomping ground. You could dig dinosaur bones out of the clay.' He rarely talks about his youth, as if he was born a man. 'It wasn't like this back then. It was unspoiled. There was a village called Stanground near where I grew up. Stony ground, where the fens ended and hard ground began. A hinterland. You could find spearheads from Boudicca's tribe, almost literally retrace the footstep of warriors worn into the earth. Now it's all retail parks and housing estates built to last a single generation.'

'It's not like you to reminisce,' says James.

'No, it most certainly is not.' He sighs. 'It made you feel part of something,' says Wormwood, trying to articulate a feeling that has resided in him from childhood without ever finding form. 'Like you were part of evolution, built up from everything that has gone before, like fish that grew feet and crawled onto the land.' He sighs. 'It's hard to explain. I don't even understand what I'm trying to explain.' He gives up.

The breeze has gathered strength and it is getting noticeably colder, but Wormwood is in rare confessional mood and they choose to stay out. 'I played Hereward the Wake in a school play, you know. He lived around here, too. He was like a prototype Robin Hood character. I got to wear a costume and wave a sword and have battles against invaders and make speeches about defending our land and fighting for what we believe in. He had some amazing adventures, fighting bears and rescuing princesses from evil Cornish tyrants. Honestly, I don't think I was ever happier.'

'I can't imagine you as a child,' says James. 'Were you happy?'

'Christ, no,' says Wormwood, laughing at his own misfortune. 'I was miserable as sin. I suspect I was just like a smaller version of what I am now, angry and disenchanted. My teachers hated me and made sure I knew it. I was too smart for my own good and cocky and confrontational. I think they only let me play Hereward so the other kids had an excuse to attack me and beat me senseless. Most of them were army brats so they had been brought up to be mean. Still, it taught me to be able to look after myself.'

James is blessed with a vividly pictorial mind and he laughs openly at the images his friend conjures for him, and especially at the thought of his friend attacking Barry with a spade.

Remember, time is a spiral, a sequence of DNA doomed to forever replicate itself.

They climb back through the window and replace the board with a little more care now that they know there is a predator on the loose. They both feel relatively well, but are old enough to appreciate that every ache and pain which assails them might quickly deteriorate into a serious issue which they lack the means to treat. To prevent light leakage which might potentially give them away, they keep the lighting low, making phantoms of them as they hunker down for the night.

Chapter 12

The following morning, Wormwood is at a loss, though not so bored that he is prepared to join in James' clumsy attempts at basic housekeeping. Floors are swept and surfaces cleaned, bins emptied and rubbish stored in lidded outside containers that will improve their quality of air without betraying their presence or potentially attract roaming predators, human or otherwise.

'I propose a road trip,' says Wormwood when James has finally stopped.

'Is that wise?'

'Probably not, but we need to do something. A person could go crazy, locked up inside all day with next to nothing to occupy them.' They both laugh at that one.

Reluctantly, James comes round to his way of thinking. 'Okay,' he says. 'I'm not totally opposed to your suggestion, but where do you have in mind?' Absent-mindedly, he picks at his fingers, an old habit he was regularly moaned at for.

'Oh, nothing too radical. I was thinking maybe we might want to go back to Peterloo, see if there's anything we can salvage. Obviously, I am grateful that you washed my clothes, but a bit more choice wouldn't hurt.' There is a gleam in his eye that suggests he knows it is a bad idea but couldn't care less.

James in unsure, but he is helpless in the face of Wormwood's overwhelming positivity.

'It will be fine,' he offers by way of guarantee. 'After all, what's the worst that can happen?'

'Ripped apart by a tiger?' suggests James. 'That would be bad.'

'Agreed,' says Wormwood, 'but I think I am a little faster than you, so in the worst-case scenario, I was planning to just let her have you so I could get away.'

'Faster?' James is aghast. 'Than me? You are deluded, my friend. I assumed you meant you were going to fend it off with your zimmer frame while I just slip away.'

They have set off already. There is very little wind today, just a light easterly to delicately pick up topsoil and carry it back out so sea. Overhead, a pair of red kites are circling. Suddenly, James sets off on what might loosely be called a run, lumbering across the uneven ground before turning his head awkwardly to mock his friend by pulling faces over his shoulder. Wormwood has never been one to turn down a challenge and he too sets off in slow-motion pursuit of his rival, his arms and legs pumping furiously to little practical effect in terms of his corresponding headway. The kites come closer, descending in graceful arcs to monitor events on the ground more closely.

Within moments, both men are in a heap on the ground, muddied but not bloodied, heaving painful lungfuls of air as they try not to succumb to laughter or anything more serious.

'Let's agree never to do that again,' gasps James. Wormwood meets his gaze but he has no breath to do more than pantomime a single word. 'Agreed.'

Afterwards, their progress is noticeably slower. Pausing for regular breaks, they make it as a weak sun is at its zenith. St Peters is as they left it, a ruined husk of a building, fallen in on itself and melted and scorched as if Godzilla himself has attacked. Hazard tape has been stretched across what little remains of the entrance, although the extent of the damage renders this futile in terms of denying them access. It is more a cautionary indicator that the building is unsafe, though they are hardly likely to let that stop them.

'Jesus,' says James. It feels like somewhere he visited a lifetime ago, a half-remembered hotel he stayed at as a child.

Time has become unreliable, a tangled thread.

They step cautiously over ruined remnants of a former life, tables where they were encouraged to create 'art' or glue photos in memory books. James is the first to notice that the dead have been removed, and he is glad of that. He imagines that they have been buried with dignity at a different location; Wormwood assumes they have been burned or dumped in anonymous mass pits, but for once he keeps his cynicism to himself. There is nothing to salvage here but memories, good and bad. Over time, it will sink into the ground, consumed by history, though future archaeologists will find nothing of interest in its ruins apart from the knowledge that in the so-called civilised societies of the twenty-first century, we thought it fit to allow our elderly to simply fade away in homes on the fringes of human dwellings, with nothing to teach the rest of us but the horrors of ageing and the inevitability of our extinction.

Outside, Wormwood stumbles across a strange collection of colourful objects elaborately bundled together, candles and flowers, like a kind of votive. Instinctively, he surmises that Ashok's family have left it, that his friend has passed on and been reborn, and that they have come to pay their respects.

For want of anything better, James agrees that it is the most likely explanation. They stand silently awhile, remembering good times that they shared in bad circumstances.

The walk, the aborted race and particularly the acrid stench of Peterloo has made it plain that the acquisition of new clothes is now a priority.

'Follow me,' says James decisively. 'I have an idea.' And off he goes, with Wormwood a step or two behind.

Sally is warily pleased to see them, explaining that the police have been there that very morning asking questions which she had reluctantly answered. Yes, her father had been there; yes, there had been a series of assaults, including one on herself; no, she didn't want to press charges, and no, she had no idea where her father might be.

The lockdown has been eased and the King has indicated in a carefully-staged televised message to the nation that the worst of it is behind them. In the coming days, people are going to be allowed back to work, to school, to go about their daily business as long as hygiene protocols are faithfully observed as far as possible. Cautiously, Sally puts her arms around her father's neck and hugs him. His grandchildren tentatively join in, the physical contact seeming awkward after so long in isolation.

His voice muffled by the embrace, James asks if her husband has been back.

'Just once,' she says, drawing back and wiping tears from her face. 'He came for money.'

'And clothes,' says the girl, Daisy. 'I had to pack a case for him.'

'He won't be back in a hurry,' says Sally. 'I gave him all the money I had. That's all he ever really wanted from me anyway. And he knows there's no more of that any time soon.'

'What do you mean? Surely you can go back to work now after what they've just said?'

She shakes her head. 'There is no work, dad. They laid me off. That's what we were arguing about, amongst other things.'

'But why? You've been there for years.' James still clings to the old-fashioned way of thinking that loyalty will be rewarded. 'You've never let then down or been any trouble.'

'I think that's the problem. Everything is to suit them. They know I won't cause any trouble and this way they don't even have to settle things with me.' Her voice is shaking with repressed anger.

'Bastards.' James hates to see her like this, but he turns quickly to his grandchildren and grimaces comically. 'Sorry about that,' he says. He turns back to his daughter. 'What can I do?'

'What can anyone do?' she wonders. 'I'll just have to look for something else. I'm sure the government won't let us starve.' But even her children hear in her voice that she doesn't sound too sure. In times like this, what work is there likely to be?

'At least you don't have to pay for me anymore,' says James. 'I can look after myself.'

She smiles sadly and takes his stupid face in her hands. It is just like him to try to stop her worrying. 'But we only had to top up a tiny bit,' she reminds him. 'The local authority paid for most of it. You're an old man. And you have to live somewhere. You need to be cared for.'

He straightens. 'I'm doing perfectly well out there, thank you very much.' He looks to Wormwood for affirmation, then back at his daughter.

'Dad, you stink. You've lost about a stone in weight. I'm amazed you've lasted this long.'

The boy has an idea. 'He could stay here,' he says. 'With us.' It's so obvious, it takes a child to think of it.

'But the police are after me,' he says foolishly, as if he is a hardened criminal rather than a lost old man.

'They're after me,' says Wormwood. 'Remember?'

James tries to recall what actually happened but he is overwrought with worry and his mind is hazy. 'I pushed him outside,' he says falteringly. 'I threw him out like the trash he is.'

'Yes, but I'm the one who hit him,' Wormwood reminds him. 'Twice, in actual fact.' His friend's expression is concerning so he tries to lighten things. 'I clonked him on the noggin. Remember?' He mimics whacking Barry over the head with a spade or shovel.

'I do,' says James. The recollection makes him smile. 'Yes, I do. It was a great noise.' He recreates the noise and his grandchildren laugh, even though the sound that amuses them is of their own father being viciously assaulted. Whoever said children are innocent?

'So it's me the police are interested in, not you.'

Sally takes him by the arm and he takes a seat. 'Of course you can stay here,' she says. 'There's nowhere else I would want you to be.' She turns to Wormwood. 'Both of you, she says. 'You can both stay here.'

But Wormwood will have none of it. 'I've brought enough trouble to your door,' he says. 'It's very kind of you, but I couldn't possibly intrude on you.' He waves away all protests. 'The police will be back,' he says. 'You have enough to worry about.'

Amongst other things, many of them considerably more slanderous, Wormwood has been described as the most stubborn man who ever set foot on the earth and there are neither arguments nor magic words to persuade him to stay.

'However,' he concedes, 'there is one thing you can do for me, apart from a nice cup of tea. I most definitely would not say no to borrowing some clothes.'

Sally laughs, glad to be able to offer some form of comfort to her father's friend. 'Come with me,' she says. 'I have just the thing.'

Ten minutes later there is a grand reveal as if this is some tawdry TV show in which the hopelessly unfashionable are restyled by so-called experts to strip the years away from their appearance.

'Wow,' says James. 'You look almost...' He reaches for the right word. 'Respectable?' Sally has taken a perverse kind of pleasure in reutilising some of her husband's abandoned clothes. He is wearing denim jeans and a smart shirt with a jacket.

The boy is trying hard not to laugh.

'Be kind,' Wormwood warns him good-naturedly.

'It's not that,' says the boy. 'You look good, honestly you do, it's just that you're wearing dad's *old man* clothes.'

'Hey,' Wormwood complains. 'When did *old man* become an insult?' He pretends to chase the boy round the room with a raised fist. 'I'll teach you to respect your elders.' Sally has to explain that Barry had thrown a tantrum at Christmas because his wife had bought him clothes he considered inappropriately mature. The boy does a passable impression of his reaction. '*I'm not a bloody old codger!*'

'Whatever is the matter with that man?' says Wormwood. 'He dressed terribly from what little I remember of him, like a sort of man-child.'

Sally wipes her eyes. 'It was quite embarrassing,' she admits. There is a communal sense of warmth which makes Wormwood pleased to be leaving his friend somewhere so full of love. It is as if a bad spell has been lifted. He senses that laughter has been in short supply in recent times, and that James' easy nature will be good medicine for them all. Though it has been many years since he has known what it is to be part of a family, he is painfully aware that sometimes the solution to a challenging puzzle is to remove a rogue piece. Without him, his own children thrived, though he couldn't tell you if that knowledge eased his pain or amplified it. Suffering is so hard to quantify, after all.

James has taken the children into the kitchen to prepare some food for his friend to take with him, whilst Sally packs a travel bag with various other unopened gifts. Essentials, as she describes them. A waterproof. Shirts. Pants. She is a little saddened by the inordinate pleasure that her father's friend is taking in her small act of charity, but pleased that there has been a small way she can express her gratitude. Her father is many things, but self-sufficient he is not. He has offered her everything he has over the years, but he has also had to lean on her more heavily than he would have liked. It is fortunate that their shared love is forged of strong bonds, that the fulcrum of their see-saw relationship has been able to bear the weight of that transition where the roles of child and parent have switched.

Wormwood is still engrossed, pulling out a razor embossed with the initials B.H. He holds it closer to his eyes to double-check what he already knows, as if disbelieving his own eyes. 'What a strange coincidence,' he says out loud.

'What's that?' Sally asks.

'This.' He shows her the razor. 'They're my initials.'

She is confused. 'I always thought your name was Wormwood. I'm so sorry.'

He reassures her. 'It is,' he says. 'Now it is. Wormwood is my new name for my new life.' She is none the wiser and he becomes aware that only an explanation will satisfy her curiosity. 'It's an old army joke,' he explains. 'I wasn't really cut out for that life. I was never great at following orders.'

When Sally pulls a not-at-all-shocked face, she looks just like her father. 'I did two tours in Ireland. The joke was that I was dead for sure. You know, wormfood. That's what they all called me. The name stuck.'

'Some joke.'

'Yeah, right. Hilarious.' She has her father's kindly face. She tries to imagine what he must have been like as a younger man, her eyes seeing through the wrinkles and scars that time and circumstance have inflicted on him. He has a proud face, but one that has had to be too strong for too long.

'It must have been tough.'

'It was, but so was I.'

'Yes, you made it.'

He looks away. 'Yes,' he says, but the softness of his voice betrays the price he paid. 'When I came out, I changed the name to my liking. Wormwood. This time it stuck.' His face brightens, his voice lifts in spirits.

James has come over to join them and has at least half-heard the conversation.

'Samsara,' he says, smiling, his hands pressed together as if in some sort of cosmic contemplation.

For a moment, even Wormwood is non-plussed but then something clicks in his head. 'Of course,' he realises. 'Why did I never think of that before?' He slaps the side of his head as if this action alone will knock some sense into him. 'Not reinvented. Reincarnated. A shiny new version of myself each time.'

James' face is old and has lost much of its elasticity, but he manages to raise a quizzical eyebrow. 'Shiny?'

'Well, tarnished. But a new version of me all the same.'

Sally has no idea what they are talking about, of course, unaware of Ashok's presence in the room with them. 'So,' she presses, 'What's your real name? Who is B.H?'

'Oh, he died a long time ago.' He carefully replaces the razor in the case. 'Wormwood is my real name.'

'At least tell me what the B stands for,' she persists.

His face betrays his uncertainty. 'Byron,' he says at last.

She has a great smile, full of warmth. 'Can I call you Byron?'

'Of course not. And if you tell anyone, either of you, I will have to kill you.'

She laughs. 'I've seen you at work with that spade. Your secret is safe, Mister Wormwood.'

'Wormwood will do, thanks all the same.' He rises and picks up the bag, testing its weight. It feels good in his hands. 'You don't want me to sound too respectable.' He sizes himself up in a mirror and is sufficiently pleasantly surprised with what he seems reflected back at him that he actually runs his fingers through his mop of hair to pull into some kind of style.

'Very smart,' she says. 'You brush up well.'

The children run into the room with an obscene amount of sandwiches which Wormwood gratefully accepts and places in his bag.

'You've been very kind,' he says, 'but I shall now take my leave of you all.' He looks directly at the children. 'I command you to take special care of my friend,' he instructs in a very formal voice. The boy salutes. 'And your mother, too.' He is of that generation that is not great with emotional goodbyes but when he looks at James, they embrace with the greatest affection.

'Stay safe,' says James shaking his hand. 'You know you're always welcome here.'

'You know where I'll be,' he says, and then he is gone.

He leaves feeling unseasonably optimistic, but the walk home is harder than he expected. Each footfall is heavy, as if gravity is exerting a stronger force than usual, pulling him down. The moon seems to hang lower and he starts to feel disorientated, unable to fully trust his own instincts. From there, once he begins to doubt himself, even the journey home becomes a challenge. Without a second person to lean on, metaphorically and occasionally physically, he is a compass without bearings. He grips the handles of his bag as if that somehow is a link to an external reality, a rudder steering him on his quest for shelter. To make matters worse, when he eventually finds what he is looking for, it takes him an eternity to find his way back in. The boards have been secured and he barely has the strength to pry them loose again and clamber through. On all fours, his strength failing him, he finds somewhere comfortable to sleep and oblivion claims him as her own.

He dreams viciously all night. Battles where sword clashes against shield and men heave and hack at each other, slipping through mud and churned earth and blood. Disembodied, he speaks in a voice he doesn't recognise, sounds issuing from his own lips that he barely comprehends, though the curses from those he is fighting are utterly alien, harsh guttural grunts that seem animalistic.

Chapter 13

Come morning, he is gently shaken awake by a face he has never seen. Exhausted, incoherent, he violently tries to pull back.

'Easy there. I'm not going to hurt you.' It is a young man, barely a man at all, wearing a uniform bearing logos that Wormwood has seen plastered all over the walls of his new home, a coffee cup with a smiling face.

'What's going on?' asks Wormwood, his voice slurred and groggy.

'You're English.' The boy is surprised. 'You were shouting in your sleep,' he says. 'I couldn't tell what the hell you were saying. I assumed you were a refugee or something.' He laughs at his own mistake. 'Or an escapee. You know, from the prison. Can I get you anything?'

'Water. Some food.'

'Not a problem.' The young man disappears out of sight, though he keeps talking as he prepares a fresh brew and some food. He has an open, friendly manner as if nothing could ever shake him. He explains that the coffee franchise is reopening, that they thought some migrants had been sleeping there, that the lockdown is being eased. He talks a lot, though the sound of his voice is a pleasant distraction from the pounding in Wormwood's temples. He is a student, though he doesn't make clear what his specialism is. Kindness, perhaps.

They eat together, and the day brightens, inside and out. Wormwood tells him only as much as he thinks he needs to know, which is very little.

'I was homeless,' he says. 'I stayed here for a little while.'

'Fine by me,' says the young man. He introduces himself as Alex. He is dark and modestly handsome, sporting a neatly-trimmed beard which is confusing to Wormwood as he has such a fresh, friendly face. 'It's just a place I work in the holidays. I certainly don't feel the need to tell anyone.' A thought occurs to him. 'Have you got a place you can stay?'

'Of course,' says Wormwood. 'Now that the lockdown has been lifted.'

Alex is unconvinced. 'Not sure I believe you,' he says. He is a whirlwind of energy, gathering cups and plates and setting about running a sink of scalding hot water. 'I can ask around. You can even stay here for a few more nights, as long as you keep it tidy. It's just me working here until the weekend.'

'Thanks,' says Wormwood, without conviction.

'Whatever.' There is a knock on the door and Alex walks over to unlock the door. He allows a customer in.

'I could kill for a decent coffee,' she says. 'It's been way too long.' Taking her complicated order, different milks and brews and toppings, Alex is too distracted discussing the horrors of instant coffee to notice his new friend slip out of the door. Suddenly, as if there has never been a lock-down, everything is back to normal. Whatever that means.

It feels good to be free. Those furtive night-time marches across fenland quickly become a thing of the past. Wormwood is at liberty to walk the streets, the first time he has done so for many months. He had half-expected it to be an unfamiliar postmodern world, something superimposed over his mental map of the streets he had first walked in a different millennium. It is and it isn't. There are times when he turns a corner expecting to walk across a park he had once frequented, pushing small children in pushchairs, only to discover a vast housing estate with identical dwellings designed for functionality and efficiency. At other times, he stumbles across a half-forgotten memento of former times, a bench where he had his first kiss, a monumental statue of a hero whose name and glorious deeds have become obscured by time and birdshit. He takes regular breaks, physically and emotionally drained by his exertions. He smiles at the thought that his life is very slowly flashing in front of his eyes. He might have expected the important moments in his life to have been the melodramatic vows and pledges, pinned medals and pioneering experiences, but what comes back again and again are the most simple pleasures, like the morning smile of a child on first waking.

The sun feels good on his skin. He is wearing lightweight cotton trousers and a polo shirt and in many ways looks no different from other people he meets on his walk. He has no idea how remarkable it is that people smile and say hello, all of them equally relieved to be free to leave their temporary prisons and socialise once again. Could it be that the inconvenience of being shut-in, that smallest slice of suffering, has made people come to appreciate the simple things? It is as if society has pressed a reset button.

A couple in their early middle age even share a sandwich with him. They exchange simple pleasantries. They tell him what a blessing it has turned out to be that social media still hasn't been reactivated. They use jargon that means absolutely nothing to him, like the men in his troubled dreams speaking in words that are alien. Further along the path in the direction he was taking, he encounters a man struggling with a panel on a lamppost. Intrigued, Wormwood stops.

'Keep walking,' the man says, without looking up at him. His voice is not unfriendly. He has pulled the panel loose and is carefully disentangling wires. He has a pair of wire-cutters on the path beside him. His mouth is open with concentration. He isolates a red wire, carefully applies the tool and snips. There is no discernible consequence. The man replaces the panel, wipes it with a cloth and then gets to his feet.

'You saw nothing,' he says, again not in an unfriendly tone.

'I saw nothing I understood,' Wormwood half-agrees. 'Do I want to know?'

'Probably not.' They find themselves walking in the same direction keeping step without intending to. The path meanders around housing estates on the fringes of civilisation where the city suddenly dissolves into greenery. These are the flatlands, but there are occasional rises and inclines that afford a slightly elevated view over the city. With weeks of respite from traffic pollution, the air is cleaner. It has been a few days since Wormwood coughed. It's amazing what real exercise and fresh air can do. For most of the walk, the man seems oblivious to the other's presence and happy to be quiet but then he can't help himself. 'It's probably nothing,' he explains, 'but there are people who says the virus was caused by radio waves from a cellular network. You know, the way we get data to use our phones.'

'I don't have a phone,' says Wormwood. The man looks at him, surprised, impressed.

'Very smart. But you know the whole world is infected with a criss-cross of invisible data-streams. There are people who claim it is harming us. Even without a phone, every step you take you are being bombarded with radiowaves.'

'And you believe this?' Wormwood has sized the man up in the way he has been trained to do. He seems credible, not uneducated.

'To be honest, I have no idea. It's probably just some bullshit conspiracy theory. But none of the other theories have made a lot more sense. You know, that the virus is a bio-weapon designed by the Chinese to take over the world economically. Who knows what to believe any more?'

'Agreed.'

'My mum died. She was fine, and then she got ill and died. And I couldn't even be with her.'

'I'm sorry.' One of his curses or blessings is that strangers have always felt able to open up to him, entrusting him with things they couldn't or wouldn't necessarily shared with those closest to them. Despite his age, his eyes are still clear and bright, great big pools of compassion.

'Yeah, well.' The man takes a deep breath and manages to compose himself. 'I just felt like I wanted to do something. They've put these 5G transmitters in lampposts so you can get a good signal wherever you are, and I thought if there was any chance that they are responsible, I could take them out.' It's a different version of Wormwood's new mantra - doing something, trying to make a difference.

'How do you know where they are?'

The man stops walking. He looks at Wormwood, checks all around in case someone is listening in and then looks away. 'Because I work for Caveo,' he says. 'This is what I do. I put them there.' He stops short of saying that he might as well have killed his mother, even if there is no truth in it. Wormwood says nothing because there is nothing to say. The heat of the sun is as soothing as the birdsong.

Instinctively, they know when it is time to move on. The rise together and walk on in silence for a short while, enjoying the sense of comradeship without having to spoil it with idle chatter. All around them, nature is taking the opportunity to reclaim every available space and the shades of green are spectacular. and then separate. 'Nice talking to you,' the man says. Tentatively, he stretches out a hand, solely becoming reaccustomed to physical contact with strangers.

'Likewise,' says Wormwood, taking his hand. 'And for what it's worth, good for you.'

'For what?'

'For doing something.' The man considers that for a moment, then nods and walks away. Wormwood stops to get his bearings. He actually knows where he is. By fate, good or bad, he is standing next to the supermarket where Sally used to work, which he knows because it stands on the site of the church where he had once sworn his marriage vows, back when religion and ceremony played a more significant role in our lives, before it was swapped out for mindless consumerism. What serendipity, that he should end up here of all places.

It is, on the face of it, quite a simple philosophy: do something. It implies that assuming responsibility for something and taking direct action is more worthwhile than simply doing nothing. Nobody ever had a statue erected in their memory for inaction, though it is fair to say that many have been commissioned for people who deserve little credit or valediction for what they accomplished in their lifetimes. Men now considered monsters with the benefit of hindsight and a new code of moral conduct. Wormwood is certain that there is a name for this idea, but the exact word for it is beyond his capacity for recall. He has no clear idea what he is about to do, but he feels a compulsion to go and advocate for the person who has offered him both compassion and support when he was in need, and who absolutely deserves to be treated with greater respect than her erstwhile employer has shown her. Words need to be spoken, and he is confident that when the time comes he will know what they are.

There is a queue outside the supermarket and he takes his place. He tries to picture where the church was in relation to where he is currently standing. It is hard to believe that a place that people once considered to be holy could fall into disuse in such a way, that hallowed ground could be disturbed and disrupted to allow for a place to buy groceries and plastic household goods. He has arrived at the entrance.

'Do you want hand sanitizer?' a woman asks at the entrance, controlling the flow of customers.

'I do,' he says. His own words shock him. Like one receiving the holy spirit, he holds his hands out flat and she squeezes out a meagre portion of liquid and mimes for him to rub his hands together. He moves on. Naturally, he has no money but there is nothing that he wants anyway. There are foot-shaped stickers on the floor to indicate which way he should go, but he is contrary by nature and single-minded of purpose so he simply ignores them and heads to the back of the store where he imagines the manager's office to be.

Turns out he is right. The door is open but he knocks anyway to indicate his presence, stepping inside without waiting to be invited. The manager is seated at a desk, phone cradled to his ear. He sizes up the intruder and is unconcerned, assuming him to be a customer with a query.

'I'll call you back,' he says, and gives Wormwood his full attention. 'Can I help you?'

Wormwood has taken an instant dislike to him. He has a manner of speaking that assumes you are wasting his time, that he has more important things to do. 'I do hope so,' he says. He starts to feel a little light-headed and would like to be invited to sit down. Good days, bad days. Which is it to be? 'I'm here about Sally. About her job.'

'Sally?' The manager shrugs. 'I need more than that to go on,' he says. He sees that his visitor is not doing so well. Wormwood reaches for the name in his mind but it is slippery, elusive.

'I'm a busy man,' the manager says with some impatience. 'Is this important or what?'

He almost has it. 'Hunter.' He defiantly returns the manager's indifferent gaze. 'Sally Hunter. She's a friend of mine.' He is a little unsteady on his feet and his voice rolls with the effort of standing upright. 'She has a family to take care of. She needs her job back.'

The manager leans forward in his chair, props his elbows on the desk. 'I'm afraid it's not that easy,' he says. 'What with this virus, we had to make some hard decisions. Times are hard for everyone at the moment.'

Wormwood takes a seat, gathers himself. 'They don't look so hard to me,' he says. 'The store is full. You must be making a killing.'

'Sure, someone is,' he agrees. 'Somewhere along the supply chain. We, however, have to do what needs to be done to make sure we survive. Sally has been a good worker, for sure, but we're not a charity. It's the hard reality of economics. We had no choice but to let her go. Tightening the belt, so to speak.' He speaks in the impersonal vernacular of the loyal lackey, doling out self-serving platitudes that render words meaningless.

Wormwood finds himself enervated by the manager's indifference. 'There is always a choice. You could do the right thing.'

The manager makes a show of regarding his watch. 'Using agency workers is cheaper. That's the economic reality. It's regrettable that we had to let Sally go but times have changed and people can't assume that a job is a job for life.' As he has been trained to do, he starts to bring the unscheduled encounter to a close. 'It's nice that you wanted to stick up for her, but honestly, there's nothing that can be done.'

Wormwood rejects the outstretched hand. 'Honest?' he says, keep his voice low and steady. 'You don't understand the meaning of the word. Is this how you reward loyalty?' He literally slaps the proffered handshake away.

The manager bristles, pulls his hand back defensively to his chest. 'Loyal?' he snorts. 'Loyal to what? A shop?' He gestures all around him to illustrate the point, a soulless pre-fabricated monstrosity that mocks the ground on which it stands. His face has reddened with indignation, his voice rising. 'All she was loyal to was the payslip at the end of the month. So she lost her job. What's that to me as long as the shelves get stacked?'

The two men glare at each other, each wondering what comes next. Wormwood is expert at uncomfortable silences and the manager relents in the face of his grim expression of disdain and simmering violence. 'You need to get out before I call the police.'

Wormwood stands dramatically and picks up the desk at his end, pushing it backwards onto the manager, tipping man and chair and desk onto the floor. He stands over him, points a threatening finger like a righteous man from a holy book.

'You will get what's coming to you,' he says. The commotion has brought other employees into the office and Wormwood takes the opportunity to slip away before he can be apprehended. There is a back entrance to the store which leads out through a staff carpark and he makes sure he is well aware from the store and anonymous before the first sirens can be heard. It has been a long day and he is not sure what he has accomplished other than to invite more unwelcome attention. It is a good half-hour's walk back to the coffee franchise and it has occurred to him that he has left his bag there.

Perhaps for that very reason, Alex shows no surprise when he reappears shortly before closing and is glad of the help when Wormwood makes himself useful putting chairs on tables and even cleaning the floors.

'You're good at that,' he says, impressed by Wormwood's easy technique with mop and pail.

'I've had a lot of practice,' he says. 'Let's just leave it at that.' He is pleased to discover that Alex has even prepared him a warm meal of sorts and they sit and eat together once the work has been done.

'Good day today?' he asks.

Wormwood considers that one for a while before responding. 'Interesting,' he says cautiously. 'I made a few friends, I made a few enemies. Same old story, really.'

Alex laughs. 'Well, either way, you are more than welcome to stop here again tonight, as long as you're out of the way by morning.'

'Much appreciated.' They chat for a while, and Wormwood learns that a degree in Sociology makes you an interesting conversationalist but not necessarily an employable one. He has a light easy-going manner and Wormwood finds himself quickly warming to him. The lockdown has had a sudden and profoundly detrimental impact on the economy and

Alex expresses the depressing opinion that he is fortunate to have work of any kind. Naturally cagey by nature, Wormwood shares only a little of his own circumstances, but enough to provoke a mixture of horror and humour in his new acquaintance.

Alex stops on his way out. 'You are quite a character,' he says. 'I just can't tell if you are the hero or the villain.'

Wormwood smiles enigmatically at that. 'You're not the only one. Perhaps,' he suggests, 'I'm a little bit of both.'

Later, he reflects on the day's events and his unedifying altercation with the supermarket manager. He wonders what he was hoping to achieve, and the different strategies he might have employed to get the manager to reconsider his actions and do the decent thing. He plays out a variety of imagined conversations in his head, playing both parts, and always finds himself arriving at the same point, with him losing his cool and resorting to violence. Is it simply that his imagination is limited, that he is blind to any point of view that is not his own? Or does the fault lie in the hardened hearts of others who are impervious to human decency and conceal their unkind deeds behind the toughened armour of authority? He has never been one to suffer fools gladly, but he has come to realise that this is a fatal flaw in his character. When faced with a confederacy of dunces, logic and common sense are weapons as crude as one's fists.

To distract himself from these thoughts which have plagued him throughout his life, and out of a growing concern that the police might be pursuing him, and out of sheer boredom, he pulls out a bottle of hair dye out of the bag which Sally has packed for him. Hardly an essential item, he thinks, but he can't think of any good reason why not.

He has never been a vain man but he is not displeased with the results, apart from the horrendous mess he has made with the public washroom. Drying his hair with his head held upside down in the stream of hot air from the hand dryer, he stumbles and falls when he tries to stand up again, but he is not harmed in the graceless tumble. He grips the disabled hand-rail and hauls himself upright, admiring his momentary victory over time in the mirror. What with his new wardrobe and the dramatic change in his appearance that comes from the erstwhile concealment of grey hair, he could almost pass for his own son. Using a brush from the bag, he restyles his hair into something that resembles a modern style based on the people he has encountered during his long day reacquainting himself with his place of birth. Like himself, it remains a place at once ancient and modern, an unhappy fusion of old and new ideas that is neither one thing nor the other. Is he an old man burdened with modern ideas, or a young idealist trapped in the ruins of a body that has outgrown him? If, like a serpent, he could shed his skin and become reinvigorated, perhaps his life would start to make a bit more sense, rather than living as he is now, simply roaming from one unsatisfactory encounter to another.

But in his failing idealism there remains something of the romantic, unwilling to accept that life inevitably has to end in disillusionment and disappointment. If this is as good as things get and there is no prospect of improvement, he would argue, then what was the point in living in the first place? He stares hard at the face in the mirror, trying to discern who it is that returns his gaze. Always a fan of the picaresque, he resolves that from this point on he will be content to live on his instincts, flowing with the currents of fate and seeing where they lead him, good or ill.

After all, if the alternative is sitting in a chair waiting for his appointment with the Reaper, then there is no alternative at all.

Chapter 14

Goodness knows what force it is that draws people to city centres, but even Wormwood has felt its pull. It is recognisable from what he once knew, but hardly. Monstrous new buildings have sprung up in the shadow of historic buildings and institutions so that it more closely resembles a theme park facsimile of an authentic English town. A variety of food franchises encircle the main square which contains a water feature sporadically spurting dirty water at unwary passers-by like some kind of grotesque game show with no viewers. Bereft of social media, unhappy families drag children around as a means of marking their release from lockdown, though one in three shops have been forced to close in the interim, leaving fast food outlets, betting ships and pawnbrokers to predominate. Wormwood notes with distaste that even the blue memorial plaque for protestors killed by the gentry during a tax protest on the side of the bank has been removed, whilst the bank itself has given way to another outlet of the globalised coffee chain that has, in effect, become his home.

The atmosphere is uneasy. For the most part, the police force has become liberalised and sanitised as a front-line force for social control, reluctant to act when required to do so for fear of causing offence or provoking accusations of being over-zealous; however, many stores and the shopping centre employ security guards who have few boundaries when it comes to doing their job. Large crowds of youths are turned away from many doors, especially those for whom English is not a first language.

'Where are you going?' Wormwood is asked. An arm is put across his chest.

He takes the arm by the wrist and firmly pushes it away. 'Inside.'

'What for?'

Wormwood conjures a face as inhospitable as the voice, especially when he sees the Caveo branding on the man's protective clothing, a serpent coiled around a tree. 'Why do you bloody think?' he snaps. 'Because I want to.'

There is a stand-off, but the guard relents. Wormwood enters but finds the experience as unpleasant as he remembered and he takes the first exit he can find. Outside, there is a commotion in a side-street leading to the main square and Wormwood finds himself involuntarily drawn to it. A sports store is being looted by a gang of youths who have stormed inside en masse and started to help themselves. A police officer has wrestled a young man to the ground over a stolen running shoe, but she finds herself fiercely berated by onlookers and decides to let him go. Wormwood wonders what he might do with a single shoe as he runs away triumphantly, but he suspects that opportunity rather than necessity is at the heart of the incident.

Another person rushes forward and pushes the police officer in the chest, causing her to fall over backwards in an almost comic fashion. The oppressive mood of mob violence hangs heavy in the air like a maddening red mist. There is a distinct instant where nothing happens and then the first man makes a threatening move towards her, presumably because her uniform has marked her out as a legitimate target in his mind. Wormwood takes a step forward and blocks the man's run, his right leg already drawn back to aim a blow at her head or torso. Despite his age, Wormwood is still a formidable presence and the man skips awkwardly to maintain his balance against the energy of his aborted assault.

'Not like this,' says Wormwood, wagging a finger. His action allows the police officer to regain her feet; instinctively, her colleagues come to her aid and they retreat cautiously, linking arms as they step backwards in formation away from the darkening mob. CCTV cameras whir away overhead, objectively capturing the incident with imperfect detail, recording some of the facts in high definition while the whole truth of what happens is obfuscated because it fails to take in the wider picture. Wormwood now finds himself facing an angry crowd he has already exasperated and frustrated. He holds out his hands and addresses them, choosing his words with care.

'Mindless violence isn't the answer,' he begins. 'You've every right to be angry, but not like this. You need to use your brains.' He pantomimes jabbing a finger at his own head. 'Think: if you are angry, who are you angry with?' He sweeps the mob with his glistening eyes. There might be twenty or thirty of them by this time. They are restless, but they stay back. 'Stealing tracksuits and trainers? What good is that going to do?' His voice has grown quieter but he still has them. 'If it's a fight you want, pick your enemy carefully before you land the first blow. That's all.'

He lowers his arms to indicate that he is not going to try to restrain them any longer, not that he could have done so anyway. Someone picks up a large stone and launches it against the window of the coffee shop that used to be a bank which marks the site of a genuine atrocity carried out by the entitled rich against the impoverished centuries before, back when people knew their enemy by the clothes on their backs. It bounces off to a groan from the crowd. It is not yet clear if this scene is going to play out as a tragedy or a comedy, or indeed both. The second time is more successful, and the crowd cheers as if something significant has happened.

That's a little bit more like it, Wormwood thinks to himself.

Like an organic living thing, the mob moves on, sometimes breaking off as people launch something through the glass frontage of a bank that has foreclosed on someone's business or to spray disparaging graffiti on the glossy fronts of restaurant chains, before reconvening as a single unified agent of destruction. Terrified shoppers scatter whilst others tut and shake fists. Wormwood does not participate in the mindful violence but finds himself helplessly swept along like a bottle containing an important message tossed on the waves of a stormy ocean, unable to catch his breath or gather his thoughts in the melee.

The sound of police sirens once more disturbs his thoughts. He finds himself pressed against the wall of a grand building and a hand grabs him by the collar and pulls him inside through a side door as the two sides violently come together. Wormwood is struggling to breathe, disorientated and temporarily blinded in the darkness. The hand is still on his collar and he is led with less force than previously down a corridor and into a larger auditorium, where the open space somehow allows more light than the claustrophobic passage down which he has just been half-dragged.

'That was close.' It is a young woman's voice, exhilarated.

'Too close.' It is a man's voice, youthful like hers but more serious.

Slowly, Wormwood's eyes adjust to the darkness and he starts to make out details, of the people who has 'rescued' him and the space which has insulated them from harm.

'Is this the theatre?' he asks, seeing with growing clarity the banked seats and aisles.

'It is,' says the young woman. 'Welcome to the place where light entertainment comes to die. The elephants' graveyard for worn-out performers and D-listers.'

'It wasn't always that way,' Wormwood responds defensively. 'I saw the Stones play here back in the day.'

'The Stone Roses?' The girl is more than a little excited.

'He means The Rolling Stones,' the man explains patiently.

'Are they that old band?' She does a terrible rendition of *Sympathy For the Devil* and a crude Jaggeresque dance. Still a little breathless with sheer excitement of the chase and her impromptu performance, she introduces herself and her partner. Isobel and Liam. She prefers Izzy.

'Call me Wormwood,' he says. He holds out a hand and she laughs.

'Wow, you're really old-fashioned,' she says. She takes his hand like a child and pumps his arm exuberantly. 'Pleased to make your acquaintance.' She laughs out loud. Liam does the same, though in a more sober fashion.

'That was quite something out there,' says Liam. He wears a beard of sorts and has a pleasant face though there is something of the rodent about him, an animalistic intelligence as if he is always trying to seek out an advantage.

Wormwood is none the wiser. 'What was?'

'The way you spoke to the crowd,' Izzy explains. 'It was something else.' She has the face of an actress, her features articulating every emotion as she speaks. He thinks he would hate to see her do despair. 'Are you a preacher or something?'

It is Wormwood's turn to laugh out loud. 'A preacher? Hardly.' His eyes have fully acclimatised to the conditions. It is a theatre he knows well, a place he has been known to frequent in his youth and adulthood on those rare occasions when an event of genuine cultural worth slips through the net of mediocrity. He walks over to the front row of seats and takes a seat.

'Why here?' he asks.

'We've been staying here through the lockdown,' Liam explains. 'When it all started, we found ourselves between homes. There are a few of us who took shelter here. So far, no one seems to have noticed. I guess it looks good for their homeless figures if they turn a blind eye.'

'Either that or they just don't care,' says Izzy. 'It seems like the return of light entertainment is not high on the list of priorities.'

'I've found myself in a similar position,' says Wormwood. 'I've been on the move, so to speak.' He realises that he has left his bag at the coffee franchise. He has never been one to care much about personal possessions, and he surprises himself with the realisation that he wants it back.

'So, not a preacher,' says Izzy. She has turned her question into a sort of game. Speaking more to herself rather than anyone in particular, she runs through some options. A politician. A policeman. She rejects all options with a flamboyant shake of the head, seemingly reluctant to move beyond the letter P in her thought processes.

'I wasn't really an anything,' says Wormwood unhelpfully.

'You didn't seem like a nobody to me,' she persists. 'You were pretty awesome back there.'

'Military?' asks Liam. There is something unmistakeable about a man who can keep his cool under pressure that screams soldier.

Wormwood returns his shrewd gaze. 'Not for quite some time,' he says. 'But yes, once upon a long long time ago.'

'Far far away?'

Far enough to have been regarded as an unwelcome alien, that was for sure, but Wormwood gives little away. 'Might as well have been.'

The others perch themselves on the edge of the stage and they talk. Wormwood asks them if they had instigated the looting, if it was pre-planned. Between them, they insist that it was a small misunderstanding which had developed into a improvised protest which had quickly got out of hand. Others had turned up and tried to turn it to their advantage.

'It's lucky you turned up when you did or people might have got hurt,' says Izzy earnestly. For a moment, Wormwood is unsure whether or not this is some private joke he is missing, but he decides they are probably on the level.

'So why did you run?' he asks. When it comes to the fight or flight instinct, Wormwood has always been very much of the former persuasion, although the fading memories of Peterloo still attest to the fact that his days of conflict have largely faded to passive aggressive battles against petty bureaucrats rather than the more visceral events which had scarred his youth.

Liam shrugs. 'In my limited experience, it's best not to get caught up in things like this with the law. Sure, we did nothing wrong, but how could we possibly prove that?'

'More to the point,' asks Izzy, 'Why did you run? You were the hero, after all.'

Wormwood scoffs. 'Hero?' It is not a word that anyone has used to describe for a very long time, and he knows better than most how hollow such words can be. Even the sound of it makes him uncomfortable. 'Hardly that.' That said, he is somewhat armed by her admiration for doing what any decent person would have done, and he decides he can trust them.

'I lost my temper with someone yesterday,' he admits. 'Not my finest hour but no one got hurt. It's been a strange few days and there are good reasons for me to avoid the police for a little while.'

Instinctively, his new acquaintances exchange glances but seem unconcerned, preferring to judge a man by his actions.

'Whatever,' says Liam. 'You are more than welcome to crash here for a while, if that helps. There is a shower and everything, and more than enough room.'

For some reason, as he ponders their offer, Wormwood recalls somebody once telling him he was like a bad seed blown on the wind trying to find somewhere to lay down some roots. Something about the mixed metaphor had appealed to him and stuck in his subconscious. He settles for a quick thanks, and then changes the subject.

'What was the protest about?'

'Oh, that's a long boring story,' says Izzy.

'Let's just say we had a little difference of opinion with our bank,' says Liam. 'They made a mistake with our account and we got charged loads in penalty fees and then we ended up getting evicted because we couldn't pay our rent.'

'And when they finally reopened and we got to speak to an actual person, they basically told us there was nothing they could do. Not even an apology.'

Liam looks embarrassed. 'So I started shouting and security guards came and literally threw us out on our arses. There was a bit of a scene and then a load of other people got involved.'

'I get it,' Wormwood cuts in. 'And then someone thought that stealing a running shoe was a smart thing to do.'

'That's pretty much the story of our day,' says Izzy.

Some others have come over to join them. They are quite the mixed bag of social outcasts; those who have clearly been street homeless for some time, others in the throes of various addictions, and yet more, like Liam and Izzy, who have suddenly and quite unexpectedly found themselves falling through systemic cracks which the current crisis has widened. All of them struggling to survive one way or another through hard times.

One of them is the man still clutching the purloined running shoe. Upon seeing Wormwood, he brandishes the shoe above his head like a prized trophy and grins crazily. At the same time, another man gets his face into Wormwood's to berate him for spoiling their fun. His breath has been fouled by cheap alcohol and vomit, and it is a small mercy that he is dragged away by Liam before Wormwood can react.

In all, there are well over twenty people congregated in the auditorium. Once the talk has moved on from who did what and who was arrested and the general excitement of the chase has subsided, the various groups start to drift apart. Wormwood spends a long afternoon listening to various tales of woe recounting how they have ended up with nowhere else to be, though he is at pains to avoid the alcoholic, having had more than his fair share of melodrama for one day.

There are two Afghans who are still suffering the trauma of trafficking, reduced from human beings to mere freight to be bought and sold and disposed of when the market suddenly fails. A solicitor's wife is taking refuge after her husband moved his mistress into their luxury home on the outskirts of the city. An ex-soldier bemoans the failure of the army's duty of care to young men who they have thrown through the gates of hell and then abandoned. Several have fallen victim to the evils of zero hours contracts, a concept that each of them has to patiently explain to Wormwood to help him understand why anyone would willingly place themselves in such a precarious position when the only party who seemed to benefit from the arrangement was the employer. Each time, the answer was effectively the same:

'What's the alternative? It was that or go hungry.'

Several others are so intent on self-polluting by means of various drugs the names of which are unfamiliar to Wormwood that they are mostly incapable of giving a coherent account of their circumstances. Bereft of past or future, they live only for the present and the insatiable need for more poison to feed the addiction, and Wormwood finds he can muster little sympathy for their plight.

The combined wisdom of the medical profession and the scientific community has failed to explain away the causes of the virus, though it is generally agreed that the worst of it is over. The doom-laden forecasts of Biblical levels of death and suffering have largely been unfounded and the biggest harm of all has been to the economy rather than to the nation's health. The failure to agree on a likely cause of the virus has led to a worrying level of insecurity, because if you don't know how it started, you don't know how – or when – it will all be over. Wormwood cannot help but think of the poor souls in St Peters who were condemned by committee to die a lonely and undignified death, quite unnecessarily as it has turned out. A cynical man might even think that the whole episode had been overplayed to rid the country of what was considered a significant drain on dwindling resources – the elderly, the chronically sick and other unproductive members of society. The junkies talk of friends who were denied access to emergency medical care, whilst Wormwood had seen with his own eyes the dereliction of duty in care homes for those who had placed their final days at the mercy of the very State they had paid into their entire working lives. The thought of it sickened him.

Local volunteers charitably supply them food that supermarkets have been unable to sell and a meal of sorts is prepared. Ironically, Wormwood learns that Izzy and Liam had volunteered for this charity when the virus first struck, and within a fortnight were reliant on the very charity they had been keen to dispense to others. It is perhaps little wonder that when *running shoe man* suggests they say grace and give thanks to God for the meal they are about to consume, it is evident that he is being sarcastic. They sit together in rows A to D, the expensive seats as it were, and Wormwood finds himself pondering the day's events. Feeling despondent and exhausted, his mind inevitably starts to wander. For some reason, he thinks of the glossy brochure foisted on the gullible visitors at St Peters, an airbrushed picture of reality that obscures any unpleasantness, the night-screams and arses needing to be wiped, and despair of people whose memories are like faulty hard drives, losing chunks of data that equate to their most precious memories until all that is left is a human-shaped husk. Each has described a different picture of hell: abandonment, insignificance, disposability, obsolescence. In Wormwood's case, it is failure, the stark inescapable knowledge that his days are numbered and that when forced to contemplate his existence, he has been unable to achieve a single thing of note.

'Is this it?' he despairs. 'Is this how everything is going to end, with everyone just sitting around and watching the world fall apart?' He is not even really aware that he is speaking out loud, his bombastic voice filling the auditorium. The sounds that come out of his mouth roll around the vast space and it is possible to discern various notes. Disappointment, naturally. No, more than that: disillusionment. It is like a spell has been broken, an enchantment that tricked everybody into thinking that everything was going to be okay, when for many people it is going to turn out anything but. The veneer of civilisation has worn thin to the point that the tragic truth has been revealed, the that the post-war generation were happy to make that Faustian pact with the devil, to live well in the present and the future be damned. Spend, consume, enjoy. Like greedy parents who sold their first-born in a gruesome fairy story.

'How can you be so meek?' he chides them. 'What kind of world will you inherit if you aren't even prepared to fight for something better?' Though he will go to his grave a defiant man, there is a slow dawning realisation that the social contract has been annulled, that altruistic belief that if you paid into society all your life, you would somehow be looked after until the end. Wormwood has reached that point when he has nothing left to lose, rock bottom, at which point anything becomes possible. From deep within his rambling mind, words form and are spoken aloud.

'Listen, all of you. You've got your whole lives ahead of you. You must want more than this for yourselves, for your children, for the people you care about.' He looks all around at him, at this mismatched assortment of people who have fallen on hard times. 'This cannot be acceptable. Things have to change,' he says. 'We can't go on like this any longer. It's time to stop being so complacent. You have to stand up and fight back.

If society tells us we are surplus to requirements, then we have to change society.'

Some of them have actually stopped eating to listen.

'If we don't work together to aspire for something better than this, something we can believe in...' He starts to lose his thread, his heart pounding in the chest, his temples. For once, words fail him.

'Together, apes strong,' says running shoe man. Somebody snickers.

Irritated, Wormwood produces a prop to prove a point, the lone running shoe. 'This,' he says, 'is not the answer.' He hurls it over their heads into the gloom where, by chance, it hits a slumbering junkie who curses foully. 'Make a stand,' he says. 'Fight back. Do something...'

Finally, he runs out of breath and stands there, scowling fiercely. He is unaware that people are staring at him. The lawyer's wife goes to Wormwood's side and hands him a drink of water. In his head, all Wormwood can hear in his own feeble voice saying: '*I can't find the words to break the spell.*' The water refreshes him as he strains his brains to coalesce all his anger into a single coherent thought. For once, his synapses align and he finds a moment of pure clarity.

'You have to stand up and fight for what you believe in,' he insists. 'Resistance is fertile.'

There is a moment of profound silence.

'Do you mean *futile?*' a voice sneers.

'He meant what he said,' someone else calls out. It could be Izzy. 'Think about it!' Angry words are exchanged and the mood darkens. The lawyer's wife has come to Wormwood's side. She sees he needs fresh air, and cautiously leads him outside, checking as she has been taught by others to make sure she is not seen as they leave the building.

'I'm no doctor,' she says with some concern, 'but you are not in a good way.' His lips are quite blue and he is almost gasping for air.

'I'll be fine,' he says finally, straightening himself. 'Well, no, actually, you're right. I'm not in a good way but that's hardly anything new.' He is touched by her genuine compassion and offers his thanks. She takes his arm and leads him away to a bench on the edge of a pathetic piece of greenery, where planted bulbs fight with litter and weeds to reach the sunlight.

'You are quite the speaker when you get going,' she says. 'Quite the rabble-rouser. My husband would have hated you.' She smiles at her own observation and he senses that she is someone who has been devoid of true companionship for some time.

'Well, that's something, I suppose,' he replies. Though straitened by misfortune, she is still an attractive woman, and kind with it, a most undervalued character trait. 'If he doesn't want you, he must be a complete fool.'

'Oh, he is far worse than that,' she laughs, though it is a joyless thing that mocks her with its own hollowness. 'The stories I could tell you.'

And tell him she does. They take a bus, and he realises for the first time that he has no money, nor means of getting any. Her name is Niamh, though for reasons that might be Freudian, he pronounces it *Naïve*. That strange sense of time travelling backwards is quite powerful. No social media. No currency. She pays for both of them, of course, enjoying the adventure. Is this, he wonders, his life starting to unravel in his final days, rewinding not in a series of quick flashes but at a more leisurely pace as befits a man of advanced years such as himself? That is certainly how it is starting to feel. Though he is unsure whether he can believes in something as superstitious as fate, it transpires that her husband works in some capacity for Caveo, the faceless corporation that seems to operate everything, from St Peters to the shopping mall to the very bus on which they are now circumnavigating the city. Wormwood has asked her if she would accompany him to the coffee shop to reclaim his bag which he is unwilling to surrender, possibly for sentimental reasons as well as pragmatism.

When they get there, Alex is pleased to see him.

'I was starting to worry,' he says, waving away the money that Niamh has proffered for the drinks she has ordered. 'A friend of this man's is a friend of mine,' he says. Wormwood can't help but feel sad that a bright young man like that with a degree should have to spend his days making coffees to pay off debts while he waits for the spark to ignite his life. Bag in hand, he feels a little happier. Alex offers them a lift when he has finished his shift and locked up, explaining that other staff will be working the next day so he is unable to stay any longer, but Wormwood is happy to catch the bus.

On the return journey, the bus is largely empty, people still wary of the invisible enemy and doing what they can to avoid unnecessary risk. It takes a different route as it circumnavigates the city and Wormwood takes some comfort in rediscovering landmarks he has not seen for many years. He opens up a little, admitting to Niamh as they pass near the ruins of St Peters that he had until recently been resident there.

She gives him a long strange look before she finds her voice. 'You really are quite the man of mystery,' she says, finally. 'How on earth did a man like you end up in a place like that?'

'A place so nice you mean?'

She scowls at him. 'You know that's not what I mean. That's where rich old people go to die.'

'Not quite,' he disagrees. 'It is for some people but that's not quite the whole story. For others, like me, it's more like an oubliette, a place where they can put you and throw away the key so you can't get into any more trouble.' She has a great laugh, but her face quickly becomes more serious.

'I shouldn't laugh,' she says. 'And you shouldn't joke about it. It's so terrible what happened there.'

His face betrays the fact that he is as surprised that she knows what happened as she is evidently surprised that he was a resident there.

'Yeah,' he says grimly. 'Tell me about it.'

'You must have been terrified,' she says. 'All those travellers breaking in to steal things. Burning the place to the ground.'

Wormwood is rarely taken aback, but this is one of those moments. 'Let me guess. Did your husband tell you that?' She nods and he takes a deep breath to gather his thoughts before putting her straight. She sits in silence for a while, contemplating in no particular order the terror the residents must have felt and a greater horror that her own comfortable existence might in some indistinct way have been funded by people who could make such a cold and calculating decision. Whatever happened to the decent man she married, she wonders miserably. Her life, it transpires, has been a near miss.

'Looking back, it all changed when he started working for Caveo,' she says at last. 'They are awful people.' She repeats the key word in case he has misunderstood. 'Awful. I had to go with him to a corporate event a few years ago in London. The CEO was there. Sir Tim. In fact, I think it was at his house. God, he was vile. He even made a pass at me when I was alone. I was almost sick. Robert never took me to another event after that.' The guileless way she says it suggests she has failed to realise that if Robert was invited to further social engagements, it was his lover who accompanied him. Perhaps he was right to think of her as Naive.

His first impression of her was that she was all surface and little substance, but Wormwood has come to enjoy her company. She has an annoying tic of constantly reapplying her lipstick, and he wonders occasionally whether it is for her benefit or for others, but she has a quick mind and a good sense of humour. Her current misfortune and loss of status clearly agrees with her, allowing latent personality traits to re-emerge.

'You wouldn't believe it,' she says, 'but I was a right little rebel when I was younger. Robert always said that was why I couldn't have children.' Wormwood clearly pulls a puzzled face because she is forced to explain. 'Apparently I was being punished,' she adds. 'By God.'

'I see,' says Wormwood, but of course he doesn't see what that could possibly have to do with anything, except to demonstrate what an absolute fool she had shared her life with thus far. When the bus arrives at the station, he absent-mindedly forgets his bag, but she is one step ahead and has it in her hand. He is irked by his own uselessness and she teases him gently for being a grumpy old man. In no particular hurry, they head back in the general direction of the theatre, though by a meandering route.

'I was quite struck by what you said earlier,' she confesses. With some effort given the inelastic nature of his skin, he raises an eyebrow for her to elaborate. 'About not wasting your life, I mean. About standing up for yourself. *Resistance is fertile.* I love it. Who was it who first said that?'

'You can never be quite sure about these things,' says Wormwood modestly. 'but I think that might have been an original thought.'

She gives him a quizzical look. 'Are you sure? It sounds so familiar.'

He laughs quietly at himself. 'I can't be too sure about anything these days, but I think it was what you might can an original thought.'

'So you're not stealing from Gandhi or Malcolm X?' He shakes his head. 'Not an advertising slogan for Nike?'

'Christ,' he says. 'I hope not. It just came to me. Let's call it the wisdom of the aged.'

She laughs out loud. 'Yes,' she says. 'Let's do that, if it makes you feel better. Anyway, you make a good point. I've spent nearly twenty years of my life with a man who clearly didn't love me. Not enough, anyway. I don't want to view it as a wasted life, but I have been doing nothing but feeling sorry for myself and I know I need to stop before it becomes a habit.' The sun is setting behind her head, casting an auburn glow around her head. 'You helped me realise that.'

They have arrived at the theatre and Wormwood struggles vainly with the side door. She shows him how; turns out there is an art to it. Chivalrously, she holds the door open for him and they slip inside, fastening the door securely as they go.

'I don't understand why you are living like you are,' says Wormwood. 'You must have money. Friends you could lean on until you get yourself back on your feet again.'

'Turns out wealth is just an illusion,' she says. 'As is friendship. He has cancelled all my cards and I have no other access to any money. I've been living on whatever I had on me when I walked out. And as for my so-called friends...' Her voice trails off.

'Turns out your friend are actually his friends,' says Wormwood, finishing her sentence when she cannot. 'I've been there before.'

'Friends.' She smiles ruefully. 'They're like sharks. They just single-mindedly swim after the next meal. If they stop, they drown. After everything I thought I knew, in the end I learned that I was just sharkfood.'

Wormwood snorts. 'And I'm wormfood,' he says. 'Pleased to know you.' They shake hands and laugh at their own misfortune.

'At least it's safe here,' she says. 'For now at least. The sleeping arrangements are a bit spartan but no-one has tried to bother me since I've been here, if you know what I mean. I've no family to speak of, so I just need a while to work out my next move.'

He nods. 'Thanks for today,' he says. He grips the handles of his bag and dreams of pulling on fresh clean clothes.

'You're very welcome,' says Niamh. 'It was nice to have some purpose for once. And like I said, those words you said, well, shouted at us, it actually helped. I am finally sick and tired of being pushed around. I think I would like to push back for once, if only I can work out how.'

'The good news,' Wormwood declares, 'is that pushing back is something of my specialist subject. We just need to work out some kind of plan.' They have reached the end of the gloomy corridor and open a door to step into the relative glow of the auditorium.

It appears that others have also been favourably touched by his words and he finds himself warmly greeted by a number of people pleased to see him return. The mood is upbeat and militant, and the conversation flies around excitedly as the diverse group of people compete for his attention and counsel. It seems that everyone has their own idea for what he meant when he spoke, which is fine by him. It is all a bit overwhelming, and Wormwood is more interested in talk of a shower than he is in listening to sketchy half-baked plans of dissent and defiance, though he is certainly pleased to see that the air of despondency which had overwhelmed the grand space on his first arrival has been replaced with something almost kinetic in its intensity. However, there is nothing like spending an afternoon in the presence of an attractive woman to make you aware of the failings in your personal hygiene regimen, and he finds himself waving them away for the time being.

Liam escorts him down a different corner leading off behind the stage to a well-appointed room with a shower, though of course there are no plush towels so after a refreshing cleansing Wormwood is forced to dry himself with his discarded clothes before dressing in fresh attire, a black shirt and jeans which are a good deal tighter than those to which he is accustomed. He feels the fatigue in his limbs ease up and the clarity of his mental processes is sufficient for him to be able to gather and organise his thinking. It has been a good day so far, which does not necessarily mean that it will be a good night.

Upon his return to the main auditorium, he takes to the stage and discusses with Liam and Izzy what can be done to ease their situation and afford them greater security. Once they have clearly outlined the problems they face, only then can potential solutions be identified, rather than simply allowing themselves to be overwhelmed by what appears to be the opacity of the looking glass in which they try to perceive their future together. Others come over to help them unravel the myriad obstacles to their problem, including Niamh, and a downtrodden younger man called Sam who once worked for an estate agency but has ironically found himself homeless after losing his job a few months prior to the lockdown. It is a diverse group of people with very different life experiences, and as the discussion develops, each person is able to look at the situation from a singularly unique perspective, until is generally agreed that the best way to proceed is to return to the bank and demand satisfaction, for that is where the fault lies. Without this resolution, it is hard for anyone to see how they can possibly move forward.

'In a way, I'm actually quite relieved,' says Izzy. 'I thought that we must have done something wrong, that this was somehow all our fault, but at least now I can see that the whole system was rigged against us.'

'That doesn't help much, though, does it?' Liam's glass is rarely more than half full, though he remains a likeable young man and a useful counterbalance to Izzy's extravagant optimism. 'What's to say we won't just get thrown out on our arses again? After all, nothing has changed.'

But something has changed. This time, they won't be going alone. Not that this is in any way a guarantee of success, they all agree, but a little moral support and a few extra hands in case things turn unpleasant again can hardly hurt. The sleeping arrangements are a little ad hoc but everyone seems to have their own space and eventually they all settle down to find what little comfort and privacy they can. Wormwood locates himself at the back of the stalls, propped up a little against a wall with rolled-up clothes as a makeshift pillow and a clear view of where Niamh is sleeping to make sure that nothing untoward is going to happen. Once he has satisfied himself that things are as they appear to be, Wormwood allows himself to plummet into that black hole growing within him to the sound of Izzy and Liam noiselessly making love not thirty feet away.

Chapter 15

The next morning, they dress as if for a party, trying to add a veneer of respectability to their mission. Wormwood shaves and even consents to pulling a comb through his hair, noticing that the stubborn grey is making a return. The plan is for Niamh to go with Izzy and Liam in the role of mother to provide an extra voice to help them articulate their grievance. Even in these diminished circumstances, she dresses stylishly and it is hard to see that a middle-aged manager of a provincial branch would not be a little disarmed by her appearance. Wormwood and Sam go along as well but wait outside to make sure that the security guard does not recognise them and make trouble, but with Niamh leading the way there is no issue with them gaining access.

As they wait, Wormwood passes the time chatting casually with Sam who is guileless and honest about the circumstances in which he lost his job.

'I was showing a client around a flat,' he explains, 'and they asked if there were any immigrants living nearby.'

'And what did you say to that?'

'I told him that Osama bin Laden rented the flat next door. It was meant as a joke. I figured it was better than calling him a racist wanker. He thought I was taking the piss and swung a punch at me. I put him on his arse and he made a complaint.'

'And that was that.'

'Yeah, pretty much. I don't regret it, though. I caught him square on the jaw.' He mimics the punch in slow motion and it certainly looks impressive.

As he sits and watches and wonders, Wormwood can't help but notice the incredible diversity of the people streaming past, much changed since his youth. The lockdown is well and truly over and a lot of people are out wandering aimlessly around the few shops that have remained open, many with too little money to be able to buy much of anything. He is reminded once again of one of his Friday night special horror films in which zombies mill around a shopping centre out of habit and a mindless hunger for live brains. There are those who might unkindly observe of the people wandering aimlessly through the city centre that they too are somewhat devoid of brains, but Wormwood has never been one to place too much value on intelligence. After all, many of the greatest injustices perpetrated by humanity have been done so by people who are widely considered to be some kind of genius, for all the good that has done the rest of us. The bank manager, for instance, who has wasted almost half an hour of his day listening to some irritating complaint from two former customers has in pride of place on his wall framed certificates from respected educational institutions signifying that he has a head full of brains, though his heart is cold and his soul threadbare. He has heard enough and brings the unscheduled meeting to a close.

'I'm sure you can appreciate that I am a very busy man,' he declares, 'and I have done you the courtesy of squeezing you in without a pre-arranged appointment between meetings, but I am afraid the answer remains the same, that I unable to do anything to help you.'

'But we've done nothing wrong,' says Izzy.

'That may be so,' says the manager rising to his feet to signal that the meeting has ended, 'But as I have explained, the system simply won't allow for me to reverse the decision that was made. Rules are rules.'

'But the rules are wrong,' says Liam, trying to control his frustration. 'The system is rigged in your favour. We've lost everything because of the decision you've made.'

A button is pressed on the underside of the desk and a security guard steps inside to escort the unwelcome guests outside. It is the same guard that unceremoniously threw them out the previous day and he knows he has the beating of Liam for all his posturing. He reaches out a paw to take Liam by the arm and lead him towards the exit.

'If you lay a hand on me,' Liam snaps, 'I'll break your arm.'

He is ignored with a mocking smirk. There is a significant size difference between them and without any kind of punch being thrown, Liam finds himself once again bundled out of the front door and into the mocking glare of daylight, Izzy and Niamh trailing helplessly behind. Wormwood has stepped forward, blocking Liam from making an unwise lunge at his adversary. He turns over his shoulder and gives Liam a look.

'Don't be so daft,' he says. He turns back to the matter at hand, sizing up the guard. The two men stare at each other malevolently. 'Big man,' says Wormwood. His voice is as flat and shimmering as fresh ice.

The guard is unconcerned. 'Big enough,' he retorts. He is probably right, although Wormwood has taken down bigger men before. He feels a tugging at his arm. Niamh has both hands wrapped around his arm and is pulling him away.

'Not here,' she insists. 'Not like this.'

Izzy is making a scene, stopping customers going into the bank and urging them to bank elsewhere. She is a force of nature and some do her the courtesy of stopping to listen to her complaints until Liam pulls her away, too.

'Come on,' he says quietly, humiliated. 'It's over.' The group reconvenes in a patch of green in front of the cathedral.

'So,' says Liam. 'That's that.'

'No,' Wormwood says. 'That, my friend, was just the start.' There is an icy tone to his voice that betrays the adrenaline pumping through his body. 'This is far from over.'

The sun is just starting to falter and people have finally grown bored of milling around and have gone in search of nourishment, the faster and cheaper the better. Wormwood is poised, single-minded in his purpose. He has been informed by one of the drug-addled residents of his latest home that the bank manager often frequents a wine bar on his way home with one of the young aspirational female employees, a fact he knows because he is the bar is adjacent to a solitary spot he favours to get high away from prying eyes. When asked how he knows it is the right bank manager, he is indignant.

'I wasn't always like this,' he snaps. 'I used to be a postman. I just into problems with the bookies a while back, that's all. Let's just say he wasn't very helpful when I went to him for a loan.'

He takes Wormwood to the appointed spot and they wait, one of them getting increasingly jittery.

'It's okay,' says Wormwood. 'You can go if you need to.'

'But how will you know who it is you're after?'

'Because he's a bank manager,' says Wormwood impatiently. 'They're all popped out of the same plastic mould. Like they are still dressed by their mothers.'

'Yeah,' the other chuckles. 'That's him all right. You sure you've got this?'

Wormwood nods. He has become aware that he always feels better when he has a purpose; maybe he has always been that way, but it is true now more than ever. His senses are sharper, though he still fatigues quickly and has periods of vagueness that last longer than he would like. Part of him hopes that the guard will accompany the manager, though he knows it is highly unlikely that the two of them would socialise, belonging as they do to very different worlds, and certainly not if the manager has clandestine intentions. Still, he has played out various scenarios in his head, settling on a choke-hold from behind that would incapacitate his opponent quickly and quietly, despite his age advantage.

Five minutes later, he is sure he has his man. He comes lumbering awkwardly down the street, at least two stone too heavy and dressed like something from a previous millennium in a polyester three-piece that hasn't fitted him well for years. Wormwood is still a little sore about the aborted encounter at the supermarket and decides to opt for a more direct approach. He steps out in front of the man and blocks his way.

'We need to talk,' he says.

'I'm not carrying any money,' the manager stutters. 'I'll call the police.'

'You don't want to do that. Just listen. You have mistreated some friends of mine, taken their money when they needed it. I need you to do what's right. Just give it back and no one needs to get hurt.'

The manager looks terrified. His face has a frantic animated quality to it as he tries to make sense of what is happening. His *uh-oh* eyes betray the moment he realises what this is about.

'Your friends. Yes, I know now.' His discomfort quickly abates once that he knows that this is a professional matter, albeit one conducted in a distinctly offbeat manner. His voice grows noticeably more assertive as it assumes the oily tone of one familiar with using platitudes to ameliorate bad news. 'That was an unfortunate misunderstanding, but there is nothing I can do about it. The system wouldn't allow me to treat their case any differently.' By impersonalising the process, he is therefore able to separate the money side of his conduct from the distress caused to individuals and therefore absolve himself of any notion of blame or guilt.

'The system,' Wormwood hisses in his face, 'is not my problem. It's yours. Fix it.' He seizes the manager's polyester tie and tightens his grip, making sure his knuckles obstruct the flow of air. 'Listen carefully. I am giving you exactly twenty-four hours to do what you should have done all along and return their money. Just so we're clear and you understand why this is important, that will be sufficient for them to get themselves back on their feet, find a place to live. Have all those things that you just take for granted. Do this, and they will close their account and move to a new bank, and that will be the end of it.'

'And if I can't?'

'There is no *can't*,' says Wormwood. 'You can do whatever you like, and we both know it. If you won't, then there will be painful consequences. Do you understand?'

The manager vainly struggles to free himself from the old man's grasp but is held fast, the fist still pressed painfully against his throat. 'Are you threatening me?'

'Of course I am,' says Wormwood. 'I'm treating you as fairly as you treat other people who come to you for help. In fact, I'm giving you a choice, which is more than you do for other people. I am not alone. We know where you work, we know where you meet your fancy women, we know where you live.'

Desperate, the manager keeps struggling. 'You most certainly do not.' Wormwood gives him the address, more or less correctly. The ex-postman knows his stuff; Wormwood can see it in his eyes that it is close enough. He stops fighting against the fist and his body slumps so that Wormwood has to take more of the strain of his considerable weight. Fear makes him stink and Wormwood knows that he his words and actions have hit their mark. Then they are disturbed by a clatter of heels. A woman has come out of the bar to see what is going on.

'Mr Thompson?' she asks. 'Is everything okay?'

Wormwood smiles reassuringly and releases him. He straightens his tie for him and restores some order to his hair in a decidedly heavy-handed manner. 'He's fine,' says Wormwood. 'At least, he will be. Have a pleasant evening.' He quickly moves away, feeling quietly confident that this time he will receive satisfaction.

Back at the theatre, someone has liberated some boxes of import beer and spirits are high.

'I can't thank you enough,' Izzy gushes.

'I haven't done anything yet,' says Wormwood, keen to limit her enthusiasm until the money is safely in their account.

'Yes,' she says, 'But thanks for fighting for us. It really means a lot.' He has grown unaccustomed to drinking and by his third bottle he is feeling a little the worse for wear, in a good way. He's not used to any of this.

'You're welcome,' he murmurs. There's something about her that unsettles him.

'Are you actually blushing behind that scowl of yours?' Niamh teases him.

'It's the beer,' he says.

'Sure it is.' She is totally at ease with him, and pushed his glass as he tips it to his mouth just to annoy him. He plays his part and scowls at her and she scowls back, then laughs at his feeble attempts to clear the beer that has spilled down his shirt.

He feels emboldened by the upbeat mood and the way the encounter with the bank manager has gone, cautiously optimistic about the prospects of fulfilling his objective and relieved that for once he has been able to avoid a physically violent encounter. Who says you can't teach an old dog new tricks, he wonders, then chides himself for his vanity.

'Weren't you afraid?' Niamh asks him.

'Of what?'

'Everything. Getting hurt? Getting arrested? I don't know.' She studies him carefully. 'You constantly surprise me. You never seem to let anything get to you. My husband was the most predictable man I ever met. In a weird way, it was one of the things I liked about him. But with you, I never quite know what you're going to say or do next.'

He laughs at that. 'You couldn't be much further from the truth,' he says. 'My life has been completely predictable. If something could go wrong, it invariably did. Whenever things were going well, as soon as I let my guard down, that was when it always blew up in my face.' He grows quiet, contemplative. She has a way of catching him off-balance. 'And the stupid thing is that I never once saw it coming.' He changes the subject. 'Your husband.'

'What about him?'

'Did you know you always talk about him in the past tense? Like he's dead.'

'He is dead,' she says unhappily. 'He's dead to me. I hope I never see him again as long as I live.'

'Hmmm.' Wormwood gives her one of his many mischievous looks, each one subtly different but all signifying trouble. 'About that. You need to know, he's pretty high up on my list.'

She falls for it. 'What list?' she asks.

He taps his head. 'This one,' he says. My mental list. Wrongs to be righted.'

She is incredulous. 'You are mental,' she laughs. 'What are you talking about, you silly old fool?'

Wormwood grows serious. 'You are my friend,' he says, 'and that means something to me. He can't be allowed to get away with treating you like this. It's outrageous.'

'True,' she says. 'But what can I do about it? What can you do? It's done. It can't just be undone.'

'No,' he admits. 'But that doesn't mean you're powerless. Or alone.'

She folds her arms around him in a surprisingly powerful embrace and doesn't let go. 'Where have you been all my life?' she wonders out loud.

They separate and she downs her beer. He has already emptied his. She yawns. 'No wonder your life is always falling apart,' she laughs. 'Has anyone ever told you that you are a born trouble-maker?'

'Just once or twice.'

The mood has shifted. Things are starting to wind down and people are drifting off to claim their place to sleep. 'I've been meaning to ask you something,' she says. 'What's that language you were speaking last night?' He is none the wiser. 'In your sleep, you were shouting out. It was very dramatic. It wasn't a language I knew. No-one else, either. I asked around.'

He shrugs. 'I can barely speak English,' he says. He has heard these same complaints before in St Peters about him shouting nonsense words in his sleep. 'I think it's just my way of annoying people even when I'm asleep. That's all I know. Honestly, I haven't a clue.'

'You were moving around, too, like you were fighting someone.'

He's been told about that before, too. 'Sounds about right. I always seem to be fighting someone.'

'Who is it?'

'Oh, I suspect it changes all the time, but I think a shrink would say it's always myself I'm really fighting.' It is a clever answer designed to bring the discussion to an end. Niamh takes it to mean he is fighting demons from his troubled past; but it could equally refer to his own mental battle with his disintegrating mind.

Chapter 16

In the morning, he wakes up cold and foggy with a dry mouth. Liam is shaking him.

'Come on,' he says with some urgency. 'We need to get you out of here. There are people looking for you.'

He allows himself to be hauled to his feet and he takes a moment to recover himself. Niamh is already dressed and has his bag in her hands. There is quite a commotion as people are rudely disturbed from their slumber. The darkness aids them in slipping away from the melee by crouching behind the seats and heading through the rear doors to the foyer.

'You sure know how to rile people,' says Niamh. Her voice betrays a certain degree of fear, but some excitement, too, as if she has slept through half her life and has found herself living a new and exciting existence that is restoring her to a better version of herself.

'Yeah, says Wormwood groggily. Liam is still bearing most of his weight. 'I told you, it's a gift.'

Adjacent to the foyer, there is a fire door and Liam opens it to allow them access to the street, and they head off as quickly as they are able towards the city centre to enable them to mingle with morning crowds. Liam has the crook of his right arm around Wormwood's shoulder to hold the bigger man upright and keep him moving but he is physically much smaller and his arm is crushing his neck. It feels like a noose tightening around his throat. Once well out of sight of the theatre, Liam leads them to an empty bench which he explains is a pre-arranged meeting point in case of emergency. Liam figures that there are enough witnesses around to provide some protection, and he is probably correct. The lack of mobile phone service has forced people to revert to primitive forms of behaviour like pre-planning, although they still have their phones easily to hand and are quick to record anything dramatic that might take place.

'I think we're safe here,' he gasps. 'Whoever they were, they definitely weren't police. They had your photo and were showing it to people to point you out.'

'Are you okay?' Niamh asks. Wormwood's colour is somewhere between grey and blue, like a defrosted cadaver.

'Not really a morning person,' he says. 'But I'll live.' His breathing is quite irregular.

Niamh disappears and returns with a bottle of water which he drinks as if it is some kind of potion with magical properties. His breathing and his colour improve.

'Is Izzy okay?' he asks, suddenly aware of her absence.

'She's tougher than she looks,' says Liam. 'And smarter. She'll be fine.' Right on cue, she comes running over to them, her face alight with excitement.

'Oh my god!' she is screaming. She throws her arms around Liam, checking he is unharmed. 'You won't believe it!' Her face is a picture of unrestrained joy.

'Believe what?'

She is brandishing a bank card, her face a portrait of sheer joy. 'I just checked. The money has been returned.' She turns to Wormwood and hugs him until he winces. 'I don't know what you did, and I don't care. You did it.'

'I'm glad,' he says. 'Really pleased.' It is a small victory, but an important one nonetheless. But at what cost?

'That was crazy back there,' says Izzy. 'Who were those psychos? They really laid into someone. There was blood everywhere.'

After a little thought, Wormwood suggests that it is most likely the security guard from the bank and his friends seeking to exact some form of revenge, and no one is able to come up with a better idea. They won't be going back to the theatre any time soon, if at all, so they sit where they are and drink expensive coffees that Izzy treats them to with her newly restored wealth.

Wormwood notes that something a little special is taking place, though you have to look quite closely to notice. An informal marketplace has been set up. People are displaying and selling arts and crafts they have made during the lockdown; artists are setting up easels and sketching, either portraits or simply for the pleasure of it. People are even using their phones to take photographs. At the far side of the square, protesters are setting up stalls with placards demanding change, though the atmosphere is more akin to a carnival than a riot. Wormwood nudges Niamh and they observe a child taking a photograph of a flower pushing up through a crack in the paving. She looks at the image she has taken and tries again. This time, she holds the camera lower and includes some broken glass on the floor that catches and refracts the slanting sunlight into tiny diamonds. She is pleased with this one and shows her father.

'This is amazing,' says Niamh. 'I remember reading that plagues often inspired artistic movements,' she explains. 'Even the Great Plague led indirectly to the Enlightenment, you know.' Wormwood raises that eyebrow again and she nudges him playfully in the ribs. 'I do know things, you know,' she says. 'I did actually go to university.'

'Yes,' says Wormwood. 'I can always tell.'

After such a rude awakening, it shouldn't be a good day, but it is. Wormwood slowly feels himself recover. Izzy and Liam head off hand-in-hand to see a friend about the possibility of a flat they can rent. Towards late morning, a young man walks over towards Wormwood, staring quizzically through tumbles of dark hair that fall across his eyes.

'I know you,' he says uncertainly.

'Yes,' says Wormwood happily. 'Yes, you do.'

The young man stares at him. 'It's you,' he says. 'What the hell happened to your hair?' He makes no attempt to stifle a laugh.
'Best not to ask,' says Wormwood. 'More to the point, what happened to your face?'

The young man is taken aback, his fingers involuntarily going to his face. Wormwood enjoys watching his discomfort. 'Your face, Jake,' he repeats. 'You're actually smiling for once. I'm pleased for you. Aren't you going to introduce me to the girl?'

He blushes. 'This is Niamh.' She is adorably pretty and embarrassed.

'Ha!' Wormwood snorts. 'So is this. What are the odds, eh?' Everyone introduces themselves.

'So,' says Wormwood. 'All's well that ends well.'

Jake is bemused. 'I don't understand,' he says. 'Is that poetry or something?'

'Yes, something like that. It means I am very relieved to see you looking so happy. Don't they teach you anything at school?'

Jake shrugs. 'Not much. I'm glad to see you doing so well,' he adds. His face drops. 'My grandad died, you know.'

'I know,' says Wormwood. His eyes express his sorrow more articulately than any words could manage. 'I was with him,' he says. 'Right to the end. He didn't suffer. He died well. Just slipped away peacefully. I wanted you to know that.' It is mostly true.

'I appreciate it, says Jake. 'Really, I do. I'll tell my dad. That will make him happy.'

Niamh stays with Wormwood and they enjoy the sunshine until the need for sustenance overtakes them and they decide to find somewhere to eat.

'Do you know everybody?' she asks him. As she speaks, she plays self-consciously with the unweathered skin on her finger where she has removed a ring.

'It might seem a bit like that,' he replies, 'but again you couldn't really be much further from the truth. In fact, I don't think my life could have been much smaller than it has been for the past few years.'

His lack of money is finally starting to become an issue for him, although Niamh insists she has more than enough. She brandishes a designer purse in front of him full of bank notes to indicate that they are well provided for.

'How long is that going to last, though?' he asks. 'Especially if you're paying for me, too.'

They have found a new café down a side-street that has sprung up in the aftermath of the lockdown, early signs that the first shoots of recovery are starting to show.

'I need to think about getting my hands on some money,' he says during the meal.

'What have you got in mind?' She skilfully wraps spaghetti around a spoon and eats it without disturbing her lipstick. 'Knowing you, it will probably involve robbing a bank.'

He pulls a mock-shocked face. 'How on earth did you guess?'

But an hour or so later, she is almost pulling that face for real when Wormwood heads off purposefully towards the bank. En route, he orders her to meet him outside the cathedral on the green in a few minutes. 'Don't worry,' he says. 'There's just something I need to do.' He falls in beside a group of people heading in the general direction of the bank. The security guard is back at his station, outside the main foyer. He is oblivious to peril, over-confident that his sheer physical bulk is sufficient to protect himself from attack, and completely fails to see the well-judged elbow that catches him across the temple as the group of people passes. Wormwood knows that it is a cheap shot, but he enjoys it anyway as he slips surreptitiously away. Live by the sword, die by the sword.

When he rejoins Niamh in the shadow of the magnificent house of God, she is relieved to see him unharmed and not swinging purloined bags of cash in each fist.

'Do I even want to know?' she asks upon seeing his self-satisfied smile.

'Best not,' he says.

'Do we need to go in and ask for forgiveness?' Niamh gestures towards the entrance to the cathedral.

'Probably,' says Wormwood. 'But I think he stopped listening and gave up on me a long time ago.'

As expected, the theatre has now been securely locked.

'Damn it,' says Niamh. 'All my things were still in there.' Wormwood is touched that her first instinct had been to grab his bag that morning rather than her own, but a little guilty, too. To compensate, he manages to force a window enough for her to climb through, though it demands a level of agility that he no longer possesses.

'I'll keep look-out,' he says.

'Sure you will, old man.' She retrieves her phone from her handbag and turns on the torch, pleased with herself for remembering to charge it while she was in the café. 'I won't be long.'

She is, though, and Wormwood starts to worry. He makes a feeble attempt to climb up and twist his body through the window, like a devolved sea-creature trying to haul itself onto land from a primordial soup. She returns to find him pathetically stuck and has to force him back out by applying a foot to push him back, letting gravity unceremoniously take care of the rest. She has recovered her bag and a few possessions but is not happy.

'Well, that was horrible,' she says. 'Someone had gone through my stuff. Everything was turned upside down. I salvaged what I could, but it isn't much.' They agree that it is definitely not safe to stay there. A hotel is still out of the question. Many have closed; the rest are full, ironically overcharging the state to house homeless people during the lockdown.

'And here we are,' she says, 'homeless and nowhere to stay. Any ideas?'

Chapter 17

The night has rendered them anonymous as they step off a bus. Like an ancient mariner caught in unfamiliar waters, Wormwood pauses to get his bearings, looks to the skies for inspiration and then sets off, Niamh a step behind him.

'Why are you still with me?' he asks, his eyes glittering. 'I'm not complaining, but it is a bit weird.'

'It's obviously not because of your natural charm,' she responds. 'I was wondering that myself. I think it's partly because I worry about you. I know you are not well, despite all your macho posturing and grunting that you're fine. I know you're not, otherwise why would you need to be in a care home getting your arse wiped. But also, primarily, it's because I literally have nothing better to do.'

'Of course you do,' he says. 'You need to go and confront that stupid ex-husband of yours and demand half of whatever he's got. He owes you that much at least. And for the record, I wiped my own arse.'

'Of course,' she says, slapping herself playfully across the head. 'It's that simple. Why didn't I see that? Just go and stand up to a big-time lawyer and just ask for half his money.' She catches up with him. 'Can you see a little problem with that? He would love nothing more than to torment me and tie me up in lawsuits for as long as possible. He can be spiteful like that.'

'I think I am starting to like him more and more each time you talk about him,' says Wormwood. 'He sounds exactly like my kind of guy.

I'm desperate to meet him face to face so I can tell him what I think of him.'

Niamh has expended considerable mental energy contemplating where her marriage went wrong, though Wormwood's wisdom on the subject extends as far as this: 'Marriage? I tried it once. It didn't work out.' She has never failed at anything, but this. The conundrum sits like a futile computer programme constantly working at the back of her subconscious mind, trying to run through obscure protocols to decode itself. She thought she was happy. Well, content, which her so-called friends have persuaded her is much the same thing when you have shared your life with someone for so long. They enjoyed each other's company, conjured up enough positive experiences to fill several photograph albums and hard drives with images that capture a life well lived. She had always imagined that was enough, that she had played her part well; apparently, it was not enough and she had been found wanting. Anger gave way to self-pity gave way to fear, and an atavistic struggle for the basic things such as food and shelter. With Wormwood's help, she feels as though she is starting to emerge from a dark tunnel and found herself somewhere else, somewhere unknown, without a roadmap or instruction manual, but not necessarily scary. It even feels at times like an evolution of sorts after years of elegant but stupefying pupation.

'You don't know him,' she says. 'He wasn't always a bad man.' She is a little surprised by her defence of him, half-hearted as it is. Perhaps it is an attempt at self-justification for the choices she has made. 'I'm sure there was a decent human being in there once,' she says. 'Now I look back on things, it feels like his work corrupted him, but slowly, you know, like a cancer.'

Wormwood doesn't respond, but in his head he can't fight the thoughts that her words provoke, a younger version of himself placed in an impossible situation, forced into making choices that hurt people every which way. He knows a thing or two about psychological trauma and the devastation that life can wreak on a good person's moral compass. They turn a corner. Wormwood seems lost but then he literally shakes his head to clear it, looks up and recalibrates his inner compass. They set off again. Almost every streetlight they pass has been vandalised, the control panel pried loose; many of them are showing loose wires, though the lights themselves still function well enough.

'Knowing the two of you as I do,' says Niamh, 'I'm not sure how well that would go. He's a big man. He spends half his life in the office, the other half in the gym.'

'Oh,' says Wormwood with a smile. 'He's gym strong, is he?' He chuckles softly to himself.

'I know that laugh,' she says. 'What does it mean?'

'Oh, nothing,' Wormwood says. He is silent for a step or two. 'It's just that gym strong isn't really strong at all. It just means he can push weights. Has he ever boxed? Studied martial arts? Has anyone ever punched him, even?'

She shakes her head, then her face brightens. 'Yes,' she says. 'I hit him. When he told me to leave.'

'A slap doesn't count.'

'Oh, it was a lot more than a slap,' she argues. 'I'll show you if you like.' She drops her bag and comes at him playfully; he drops his bag and fends her off with ease. He grabs her wrists in a single paw and it is over.

They are close. Wormwood counts off the numbers and then knocks at a door. Sally's face appears and she smiles in recognition.

'It's you,' she says warmly. 'You'd better come in.' She steps aside to let both her guests across the threshold and looks up and down the street before closing it. 'Dad,' she calls. 'Visitors.'

James emerges from the living room and embraces his old friend.

'You're looking good,' says Wormwood.

'Look who it is!' says James. 'It's public enemy number one! And who's this you've caught up in your latest misadventure?'

'Niamh,' she says, introducing herself. 'I'm his carer.' She puts out her hand.

'You are bloody not,' says Wormwood. 'I'm your carer, more like.'

Sally puts the kettle on for a brew whilst James fills them in on the latest developments. 'The police have been around again,' he explains. 'Let's just say they are quite keen to catch up with you for a chat. Who on earth have you been upsetting this time?'

It says a lot that Wormwood has to think for a while before he can disentangle each incident to choose which of his recent adventures is most likely to have provoked the release of the grainy but unmistakeable photograph of him inside the most recent edition of the local paper. It accompanies a vague article about a man wanted in connection with an incident in the city centre.

'What are you like?' says James, exasperated but clearly also relieved that his friend has lost none of his power to astound. 'To be fair, the police actually seemed to be on your side, if anything.'

Niamh relates the story of the looting and Wormwood's timely intervention.

'That is so bloody typical of you,' says James. 'Always trying to do the right thing in the wrong place.'

Sally comes back in with a tray of tea and cakes. She seems lighter somehow, though the involvement of the police is clearly causing her some anxiety, as is having her father to care for. She explains that she has got her old job back, sort of. She received a call from someone from Head Office offering part-time work in a different store a lot closer to home.

Wormwood smiles enigmatically. 'I'm really pleased to hear that,' he says.

'It's not ideal,' she says. 'I'll probably have to get someone in to look after dad while I'm working when I get my hours sorted out, but at least I'll be able to put some food on the table. And this time there is absolutely no way that I am going to send him to live in some godforsaken home for strangers to look after.' James had always sworn that it was only at Barry's insistence that he was moved into St Peters. His daughter sobbed for a week.

'Maybe not,' James insists. 'I'm actually doing pretty well since I, you know, escaped.' He still struggles to find the right word to describe the end of his stint in the care home. 'I even did some wiring work for a neighbour yesterday. I feel so much better to be useful and active than I ever did in St Peters.'

'Who knew?' says Wormwood. 'It's like we were put there to fossilise.'

They crack a bottle of cheapish red wine and spend a pleasant evening together. James offers them a place to sleep for the night when they explain that, once again, they are temporarily homeless.

'I just wish I could offer you something more permanent,' says Sally.

'I wouldn't hear of it,' Niamh reassures her. 'We'll be sorted out by tomorrow, but it's very kind of you.'

They go off to sort out some air beds and blankets and James takes the opportunity to quiz his old friend. 'Did you have something to do with her job?' he asks. 'I saw that look.'

'I don't know what you mean,' says Wormwood unconvincingly. 'I might have gone for a shop and had a quiet word with someone about job vacancies, but nothing more than that.'

'Shopping?' says James with a grin. 'With what? Magic beans?'

It feels good to be together again, and he is quietly reassured that Wormwood doesn't look quite so terrible as he would have thought. He does look tired, though. He has to work quite hard to reassure James that he is taking some care of himself.

'Whatever you did,' says James, 'and I honestly dread to even think about it, I can't thank you enough. I wish there was more I could do.'

'I'm fine. The best thing you can do for me is just to stay here and be loved and taken care of. That's all. I've got a few things to take care of, and then I can start to think about settling down to the quiet life.'

'The quiet life? You? That didn't work out quite so well last time.'

'True enough,' says Wormwood. 'But things are different now. It might be a little late in life, but I think I might actually have found my purpose.' He sees the look that James gives him, that poker face that always gives everything away. 'Don't worry,' says Wormwood sincerely, 'I'll be fine. Once I've got Niamh straightened out and everything is as it should be, I think I'm finally going to be able to find some peace at last.'

Whatever that means.

Chapter 18

Morning breaks with a glorious sun which seems to intensify everything it touches. Wormwood wonders at first if he is having some kind of episode as he stands and stares out at a garden filled with the most vibrant colours. Sleepily, he rubs his eyes but he wakes up feeling as good as he has in a long time. Refreshed. Revitalised.

Niamh comes downstairs and walks over to stand beside him.

'It's the rain,' she explains. 'This is what you get after such a drenched winter. It's lovely, isn't it?'

'Yes. It's quite something.'

Sally is in the kitchen preparing a breakfast. James stumbles downstairs with a grandchild attached to him. They eat well and the talk comes easily across the table, though Wormwood is vague about his plans.

'We'll have to see,' he says more than once, being uncommonly evasive.

By mid-morning, it has been agreed that they will stay for an extra day. Sally has a full day of work ahead of her stretching into the evening, and Niamh insists that she stay to help look after all the children, in which she playfully includes the two elderly gentlemen. They spend a lazy day together lounging in the garden, drinking slowly and happily whilst James embarrasses his friend and entertains all the others with tales of Wormwood's mischief in St Peters. Sometimes they rock with laughter; at other times Niamh slaps Wormwood for being so unkind.

James is wiping his eyes. 'Do you remember when we all pretended to have ebola?' He turns to Niamh. 'We even had blood dripping out of our eyes. Amanda went crazy.'

'That was your idea.'

'No, I think you'll find it was yours,' says James. 'It was always you. The ringleader.'

Wormwood strains his memory. 'Actually, he says, 'I think that one was Windrush. That was his forfeit for losing at poker again. He had to come up with the next idea.'

'Okay,' James conceded. 'I'll let you off for that one. Good old Windrush. I bet he's having a hell of a time wherever he is.'
They go quiet for a moment, smiling at the remembrance of their friend.

'What about Halloween!' They laugh so hard that they get nowhere close to being able to tell the story. The children laugh, too, not really knowing what is so amusing but enjoying the general fun mood.
'Honestly,' says Niamh. 'I think I would have smothered you all with your pillows as you slept.'

'I think it did her mind more than once,' says James. 'But she was a nasty piece of work. She had a real mean streak to her when she was in a bad mood. I never really felt sorry for her.' He thinks about that for a moment. 'Well, sometimes, for a bit, but then she was a mean bitch again and deserved everything she had coming to her.'

'Grandad, you said a bad word.'

He blushes apologetically.

'He meant witch,' says Wormwood unhelpfully.

Niamh slaps him across the head. 'Sexist!' she scalds him. 'She sounds like a poor woman mercilessly bullied by naughty old men who should know better.'

'All I can say, says James, 'is that you obviously never met her.'

'She was a born monster,' says Wormwood, recalling the unpleasant circumstances of their last meeting. 'We didn't make her that way.'

Wormwood goes to the toilet and James takes the opportunity to talk openly to Niamh. 'How's he doing?' he asks. 'It's weird, but I feel so much better since I came here with my family, but I know things are very different for him. Is he still having spells where he is vague, when he isn't really himself?'

'He is,' she says. Her eyes subconsciously flick upwards to try to discern a pattern. 'But not often. He gets tired, but so do I, to be honest. It's not easy out there. I think he's doing okay. I'm doing what I can to keep an eye on him.'

James gently touches her arm. 'I can see that,' he says warmly. 'I can't thank you enough. I know he's not easy.'

She mirrors his smile, enjoying the understatement. 'No need for that,' she says. 'It's been a riot. I've never had so much fun.'

'Yes, he is quite something. Back in St Peters, he had entire days when he believed he was some kind of ancient warrior-king. He drove the staff crazy. He would wake us up sometimes with battle-cries all through the night.'

She laughs in recognition. 'That explains a lot,' she says. 'But honestly, he's pretty lucid at the moment. I think it helps that he has a mission, something to provide some focus. He's on a mission.'

'Something positive too channel his energies. Yes,' he says. 'I'm not entirely sure what he thinks his mission is exactly, but I do see that.'

'Yes, he is a bit vague about the details but he basically sees himself as the righter-of-wrongs, trying to save the world, one needy person at a time.'

'That's it,' exclaims James. 'Of course. I can see what this is now. It's become a classic Old Testament vengeance mission.' He makes the sign of the cross, badly. 'Heaven help us all.'

'Amen,' she adds. Her voice drops to a whisper as Wormwood returns. 'What are you two gossiping about?' he asks sharply.

'Its's funny you ask,' says Niamh. 'We were just discussing handing you over to the authorities and claiming the reward.'

'You wouldn't dare,' he jokes, shaking a fist. 'You both know they'll never take me alive.' Then he reconsiders, grows pensive. 'Although,' he says, 'we could do with the money...'

Later that day, something in the latest edition of the local paper grabs their attention.

'You're not going to believe this,' say James.

Next to an article about anti-social media and the rebirth of face-to-face conversation, there is a follow-up article illustrated by the same photo of

Wormwood clarifying the request for information from the police. James reads it aloud. There is a quote from the police officer admonishing the newspaper for the tone of the article and defending the man who had saved her from harm and the implication that he had in any way been responsible for the looting or vandalism. There is a letters page in which various people have written in, witnesses to the incident standing up for him or other respondents linking him to a former resident of a care home who matches the man in the photograph.

'Wow!' says James. 'I think you're famous.'

'Infamous is more like it,' Niamh corrects him. They each take turns reading the letters and share notes, trying to work out the best way to proceed. James suggests he hands himself in at the local police station so the misunderstanding can be cleared up. Without giving too much away and creating undue anxiety for James, Niamh hints that their recent escapades might have blurred the issue a little. She fails to openly mention the small issue of the bank manager and how that escapade might complicate things if the matter has been formally brought to the attention of the authorities, but Wormwood is able to infer the meaning behind her words.

'What am I going to do?' he asks the room rhetorically. 'I guess I'm going to do what I've always done. I'm going to just keep moving. I don't trust anyone enough to believe that the truth will out and that justice will be done.' James makes a half-hearted attempt to change his mind, but he knows that his friend is probably right.

A few minutes later, the decision is taken out of their hands anyway. There is a knock at the door. James is upstairs putting his granddaughter to bed but he comes downstairs and answers.

'Mr Hunter?' a voice inquires. 'Can I have a word?' The tone of coice makes it clear it is not up for debate.

'What's this about?'

'It's about a former acquaintance of yours. Can I come in?'

The man at the door is a big physical unit but James blocks his way. 'I'm putting my granddaughter to bed,' he says, trying to keep his voice steady but also loud enough for Wormwood to be able to hear. 'What's this about?'

'I told you,' the man says, his tone noticeably less amiable. 'An acquaintance of yours. Mr Wormwood. I understand you were recently in a care home with him. Is that correct?' He tries to step inside the house but James physically blocks him.

'Sorry,' he says. 'I can't help you. You need to go.'

'I just need an address,' the man says. 'I don't want any trouble.'

'There won't be any trouble,' says James. 'You just need to get off my property. I told you I can't help you and that I'm busy. If you don't go, I will call the police.'

The man sighs. 'This isn't over,' he says. 'I know you know something. I will be back and next time I won't be so nice.'

'You haven't been nice this time,' James snaps back at him. 'Now fuck off.'

The man stands and stares as James slams the door on him and fastens a chain that is laughably flimsy compared the to the powerful bulk of the man who has not moved an inch. He holds his breath and expects the door to come flying open at any moment but the man clearly weighs up his options and decides against escalating things. He says something incomprehensible through the door and skulks away. James goes to the kitchen to check on his house guests but is hardly surprised to find that they have already slipped away unnoticed through the back garden. What he doesn't know is that Wormwood has safely stowed Niamh somewhere safe and then double-backed just in case things have got unpleasant. Shrouded in shadow, he makes sure the man has gone before he makes his way back to Niamh.

'Goodbye, old friend,' he says, knowing that he has probably seen James for the last time.

Chapter 19

They are sitting in a retro café in a highly respectable village where the only sign of the city to which it is loosely attached is a silhouette of the cathedral far off into the distance. Usually it is concealed by pollution, but people have remained strangely reluctant to take to their cars since the lockdown has ended, almost as if the act of driving to and from work was part of a terrible dream from which they have awoken. They are mid conversation.

'I just don't understand why you were ever in a place like that.' The light sparkles in her eyes.

'Me neither.'

'You know what I mean. A residential care home? You?' She puts her head in her hands. She has dressed up for the occasion, her hair skilfully arranged to show off her high cheekbones. 'It was never going to work.'

He shrugs. 'I guess there was no better option.'

'But you must have been somewhere better before that.'

He studies her face carefully. She has shrewd eyes and is clearly very bright but she doesn't ever seem to ask quite the right question, as if she is constantly evasive of a deeper truth she is not ready to hear.

'Why must I?'

'Because it's hard to imagine anywhere worse, that's why.'

'Let's just say I wasn't left with a lot of choice.' He is not forthcoming with more information so she lets it drop at that. When you reach a certain age, you begin to appreciate that there is no commodity as precious as time, though currently that is perhaps the one thing that they are not short of; however, he still can't raise the enthusiasm to explain the circumstances which led him to being incarcerated. Money they are getting short of, however. They order carefully, tea for two and Victoria sponge.

'What about you?' he asks. 'You're always so interested in me, but you never really speak about yourself.'

His habit of shrugging is apparently infectious. 'There's not much to tell. You already know most of it. I worked for a while, and they I got married and then I didn't work. And then I got unceremoniously dumped and then I met you and then I got into endless trouble for no good reason.' She stops and smiles at him disingenuously.

'What did you do when you didn't work.'

'Honestly,' she says,' I can't remember. I'm ashamed to say I even had a cleaner. I just did...stuff.'

'With your friends who it transpired weren't really your friends.'

This time her smile is genuine, though tinged with sadness that turns down the corners of her mouth a little. 'When you put it like, it all sounds a bit pathetic. But yes, pretty much.'

He continues to probe. 'And what did you study?'

'That's an easy one. Psychology and Law.'

He laughs loudly enough for heads to turn. 'And now here you are on the run with a wanted felon with an oppositional personality disorder! Ha!'

'On the run?' she teases. 'You're running days are long behind you. Can you be *on the run* with a zimmer frame?'

He stares at her with false earnestness. 'Are you sure you weren't a comedian?'

She ignores him and continues. 'So, then I became a legal secretary for a law firm, and Robert worked there and was on his way up. He used to want to do good things but there was never any money in it and I guess he just sold out for an easier life. I guess it all seemed like such a good idea.' Her voice trails off into uncertainty, still trying to make sense of where her life has gone.

'Bad ideas often start out like that,' says Wormwood. 'It's something I've become a bit of an expert in. They disguise themselves as good ideas, and they can be really convincing for a while, and then, when you least expect it, all the glitter falls off and you realise you've messed everything up again.'

'Maybe it is fate,' she says. 'We are quite the pair of losers, aren't we.' She takes an enormous bite of cake so that buttercream and jam explode comically out of the sides. Someone at an adjacent table tuts and Wormwood makes eye contact and then does exactly the same.

The next thing they know they are standing outside a mock Tudor mansion that might actually not be mock at all.

'Are you kidding me?' says Wormwood. She nods apologetically, though what she is apologising for is not clear. In fact, they are standing across the road from the house on a tree-lined street, furtively concealed behind a grand oak with obligingly low growth that has not yet been cut back. Though he has not known her for long, they have been through some quite difficult situations, but he has never seen her look so nervous.

She looks at him with frantic eyes. 'I can't do this,' she says.

'Yes,' he says. 'I know you. You can do anything.'

'Not this,' she repeats. She stresses the first word. '*This* I cannot do.'

His eyes sparkle warmly. 'Yes,' he says. 'This yes can you do.' He holds her by the shoulders. 'The way he has treated you is appalling. All you are going to do is go in there and make him give you what is rightly yours. Being a lawyer doesn't make him right. You know the law. You've studied it. Half of this is yours. So you can stand on your own two feet and become the person you want to be and not the person he wanted you to be.'

'And then decided he didn't even want.'

Her voice has become more militant, which is exactly what he was hoping for. 'Exactly.'

Maybe for dramatic emphasis or to summon up the courage to do what must be done, they wait for the light to begin to fail before they make their move.

'Keys,' he demands. He holds out his hand.

She stops dead in her tracks. 'I don't have them,' she says. 'He took them off me, or I threw them at him. House key. Car key. The lot.' She expects him to turn around but he is resolute.

'Never mind,' he says. 'We'll just have to improvise. I'm expert at that.'

She grabs his shoulder to hold him back. 'You are not,' she says, instinctively dropping her voice to a hissed whisper. 'You think you are, but you aren't. You are an expert at only one thing, and that is getting into trouble.'

He pushes on to the boundary of the house, looking for a gap in the hedge to gain access to the garden. A security gate prohibits unwanted access to the house via the main driveway so he has to seek an alternative means of egress. After a short while, he is able to physically manhandle her through a break in the foliage and they walk up to the house from the rear. Surprisingly, there are no security lights.

'Robert always said that lights were crude and polluting,' she explains. 'He swore that he was more than capable of dealing with any trespassers if it came to it.'

Wormwood rubs his hands. 'Well, maybe we'll have to see about that.'

They try the back door which, unbelievably, is unlocked. Talk about complacent. As Wormwood places a hand on the handle, she puts her hand on his.

'Seriously,' she says, 'I can't do this.'

'It's a bit late to turn back now.'

'It really isn't.' She shakes her head emphatically. 'All we need to do it turn and go back the way we came. No-one would ever know we were even here, trespassing.'

'You can't trespass in your own home.' He grabs her by the shoulders and gives her a gentle shake. 'Come on,' he says. 'Death or glory!' And he steps inside. She waits, counts to three, to five, to ten and then the suspense is too much and she follows reluctantly after him, cursing him with every step she takes. He hasn't got far. She finds him stretching out his arms, flexing his body.

'What on earth are you doing, you crazy old man?' she whispers in a hiss.

'Preparing myself,' he replies. 'Getting ready in case things get messy.' Gorilla-like, he pounds his fists against his chest. 'To get the adrenaline flowing,' he explains in response to her quizzical look.

'Stop it!' she commands. 'You look like a madman and you'll give yourself a heart attack.'

The room is dark, spacious, tastefully appointed with furniture that creates a modern minimalist vibe that is probably very much *en vogue* for people who read the right magazines. Somewhere a light turns on and a faint glow illuminates the space under the door.

'Niamh?' says a tentative voice from outside. They had braced themselves for a roar and thunder, but this is something very different. The door opens tentatively and a figure steps inside, a back-lit silhouette that almost fills the frame. 'Is that you?' The voice breaks with emotion.

A hand fumbles against the wall and the light comes on. They form a bizarre triangle within the room as the figure steps inside. Wormwood stands square on, fists clenched and ready for whatever comes at him, Niamh has her arms folded defensively across her body, her husband standing foolishly in silk pyjamas, all of them roughly ten feet apart, the classic Mexican stand-off. Suddenly, Robert lunges at Niamh and she lashes out wildly and catches him in the groin. He crumples and falls heavily across the polished parquet flooring. A barely audible sound emanates from his mouth which is scarcely human. He remains prone for some time, like a gargantuan foetus curled in on itself protectively. Finally, he finds his voice.

'What was that for?' he gasps.

'Because you lunged at me. It was self-defence.'

He struggles to his knees. 'Fair enough,' he says. 'But I was trying to embrace you. I've been such a fool.' He can barely look at her, but he can't take his eyes off her either; he adopts a crouched stance, making himself seem less threatening, apologetic almost. She is quite taken aback, disarmed. There is nowhere for her fury to go. Wormwood instinctively takes a couple of steps back, suddenly feeling like a redundant chaperone.

'What exactly are you saying?' She notices that he looks terrible, and this a man for whom the word vanity is a bespoke fit. Normally, his hair is perfectly manicured with side parting and just the right amount of body to set off the squareness of his jaw; tonight, it is plastered inelegantly across his brow.

'I'm saying sorry,' he stammers. 'I can't believe what I've done to you, treating you like this. I can't say it enough times.'

'You possibly can,' says Wormwood unhelpfully. She turns and glares at him.

'I don't understand,' she says, suddenly feeling like a character in one of the sentimental melodramas that her so-called friends mistake for literature and insist on giving her to read. 'What's happened to you? Why are you being like this?' She is unconvinced by his self-pity, never having been one to buy into the fallacy that pain is proof of love.

He moves towards her again and she backs away. 'I am so sorry,' he repeats. 'I am so ashamed of myself. I haven't slept. I've called all our friends and no-one could tell me where you were.' To be fair, he does look half out of his mind with worry. His face is bruised and sore. 'I have literally been beating myself up.'

'Poor you,' she says, though not in a kindly way. 'Is that supposed to impress me?'

The room falls silent. You can see on his face that he is trying to conjure the words to make things all okay again, as if life is ever that simple outside of children's picture books and cheap melodramas. There is a frenzied quality to his features that reveals the extent of his suffering.

'It didn't have to be this way,' she says, 'but you made a choice, and it wasn't me.'

His head drops to hide the tears that well in the corners of his eyes. Salty drops splosh on the intricate flooring. 'I was wrong,' he says. 'I know you won't ever forgive me.' From his knees, he looks up at her and she is overwhelmed by a desire to kick at him. 'I went looking for you every day,' he pleads. 'Every day, everywhere I could think of. I couldn't bear it.'

'And yet here you are. You could bear it.'

'Barely,' he says, desperately. 'I had to come back every night in case you miraculously turned up.'

'Yes,' she says. 'And now here I am.'

'It's a miracle,' says Wormwood under his breath. Hallelujah!

Robert turns to him. He looks almost deranged. 'And who the hell are you?' he asks. He sizes Wormwood up ungenerously in case he is some kind of unlikely love rival, then turns to Niamh accusingly.

'Seriously?' she says. 'But while we're on the subject, where's the whore?'

Robert blinks at her uncomprehendingly for a moment and then understands. 'Annabel?' he says. 'Here? Never. She meant nothing to me.' He pulls himself together to do sincere. 'She is history.'

'So,' says Niamh. 'It's Annabel, is it.' The name means nothing to her, but now the source of her pain has a name, as if a physician has finally provided a latinate medical term for a malignant tumour. She sits down heavily in a chair which is absurdly comfortable. There is no sound apart from the emotional heaving of Robert's despairing breath, two lovers trapped inside their own solitary bodies.
Wormwood suddenly feels very much out of place and turns to go.

'Wait!' Robert's voice stops him in his tracks. He is obviously used to being obeyed. Part of Wormwood's oppositional personality wants him to resist, but he decides to see what Robert has to say for himself.

'I want to say thank you,' he says, 'for keeping her safe.' Given his profession, it is hard to know whether he is being sincere but against his nature, Wormwood is inclined, on this occasion, to be generous. 'I have stared hard into the mirror,' he continues, 'and to be frank with you, I have not liked what I have seen.' To be fair to him, it is not hard to imagine him staring at himself in a mirror. He has a face which is almost absurdly symmetrical and the kind of toned physique that alpha men of a certain age imagine adds to their aura of invincibility. 'This whole business with the pandemic has really shaken me, forced me to reconsider my core values,' he confesses. 'I know how shallow that sounds, but it's the truth. Some of the things I am being asked to cover up you wouldn't believe.'

'He was actually at St Peters at the end,' Niamh cuts in, gesturing towards Wormwood who is standing uncomfortably to one side. 'You aren't going to be able to shock him.'

'You were working there?' says Robert incredulously. 'The whole affair is scandalous. I know at the time we thought the virus was going to be far far worse than it has turned out to be, but that is no excuse for what happened.'

'Tell me about it,' says Wormwood.

'Robert, he was a resident there,' Niamh explains.

Robert literally does a double-take. He sizes Wormwood up and can make no sense of it. 'But that's absurd,' he says. 'That can't possibly be true.'

Wormwood holds out his hands. 'I buried people with these hands,' he says. 'I don't care whether you believe me or not. Either way, it's the truth.'

Robert is clearly suffering some sort of existential crisis. He has crazy eyes, flicking back and forth between the two of them. 'This is not who

I thought I was going to become when I first started out,' he says. 'When I started out, I actually intended to only take on ethical cases, if you can believe that.'

Wormwood gives him a look which implies that he does that he does find that a little hard to believe, and he looks away.

'Anyway, I'm releasing documents to the press,' he says. 'I can't be a part of this anymore, whatever the consequences. People are already kicking up a fuss, at the highest levels. Caveo are in real trouble. Their share price is plunging. Even the PM is involved.' This time, he looks directly at Wormwood. 'I can't change what happened, but I can promise you this: even without my intervention, heads will roll for this.'

Wormwood nods. 'I think I'm going to leave you two to it,' he decides. He bends and picks up his bag. His work here is done. He has no idea how this is going to play out, but he is satisfied that Niamh has the whip hand and is in a mood so brutal that she is going to be nobody's fool. Whether they reconcile their differences or not makes no bones with him. He is hardened to the fact that he is on the path to hell, but everyone has to be free to make their own choices. He would have it no other way.

At the doorway, Niamh catches up with him. 'Thanks.' She kisses him on the forehead.

He smiles at her. She has never looked more composed, in control. 'I think you can take it from here. Do you know what you need to do?'

She nods, wiping away a stray tear. 'I do,' she says. She presses something into his hand. 'You're going to need this,' she says. She stands in the doorway and watches him slink away to be swallowed up by the darkness like a hushed-up secret that will eventually find its way into the light of day.

She cups her hands to mouth and calls out after him until even his shadow has disappeared.

Reluctantly, she closes the door and leans against it for support.
'Give them hell, old man.'

Chapter 20

He is on the move again, almost as if he is afraid to stop. The evening is clear and fresh and a fullish moon sits heavily in the sky a little past its prime. When Wormwood looks at it for inspiration, he imagines he can see the scars of ancient rivers amidst the pock marks of cosmic collisions, though it is more likely that what he can see is the result of his failing eyesight, random blood cells passing in front of his retina that look like phantom lunar features. His mind wanders with each stride, thinking about Friday night film sessions at St Peters. He recalls James loudly complaining that post-apocalyptic films always involve the survivors just wandering aimlessly from one life-threatening scenario to the next, a plot device he found both predictable and frustrating; now it seems like the writers were modern seers, anticipating the pandemic and Wormwood's nomadic existence. Who would ever have guessed it for a man whose world had been reduced to four walls, a toilet and a garden? He feels glad he watched these films so avidly, all the better to prepare himself for the trials and tribulations he has passed, and those that still await.

At least he isn't cold or wet, although he has only a vague notion of where he is heading. He has come to see his faulty memory as a kind of roadmap to a place he once knew well. The colours have faded and creases now obscure parts essential in order to see the individual parts as a coherent whole. What saves him is that he is self-aware enough to know he is struggling. He can almost feel the synapses misfiring like tiny pops in his head, which might explain his habit of rubbing his temples furiously when his mind starts to go foggy, as if by doing so he can compel his temporal lobes to do their job. Otherwise, he is becoming a photograph of himself that is starting to fade, a ghost of himself.

His legs are strong and his sense of injustice grants him boundless spirit to keep going. But go where? The address Niamh has scribbled on a piece of paper wrapped up in a bundle of banknotes is meaningless to him, a cul-de-sac he has never heard of on an estate he didn't know even existed. Not a part of his known world, the letters mean nothing to him, like indecipherable hieroglyphs. He does the best he can. He walks towards the unknown, at every turn taking the unfamiliar path. A strange new logic has crept into his thinking: if he is trying to find a place he doesn't know, then he has to forget what he knows and head in the opposite direction. He feels like a character in an ancient riddle, a tale told through the ages to instruct the ignorant in how to become wise. There is barely any space left in his thoughts for Niamh. She is stronger than she knows and he trusts that she will do what is right.

Now all his friends have gone, but he does not feel alone. There are voices in his head. Perhaps they have always been there but now they can come through more clearly, like an analogue radio than has finally been tuned. He can distinguish Niamh's voice in the mix, gently mocking but full of compassion; and James can be heard, though less distinctly, and the bass notes of Windrush, and others, too, everyone he has ever known and cared about and fought for. Their voices coalesce into a single narrative, like an urgent whispered chant, urging him on, to keep going, to demand satisfaction, for all of them, for all of us, everywhere.

In the moonlight, his eyes are certainly glittering now. He looks magnificent, like an ancient primordial bear on an epic hunt. On the path ahead of him he sees a group of youths smoking weed, seeking refuge in a fug of their own smoke. The pungent aroma reminds him subconsciously of Windrush, his old partner in crime, and he instinctively smiles. One of them has smudges of colour across his upper lip and is brandishing a can of spray paint, his eyes red and faraway.

'There are better ways to use that,' says Wormwood, regarding the can. Still grinning, like a man not in full possession of his senses, he approaches them wordlessly brandishing the piece of paper. They look at him with awe, this hulking preternatural creature, and they do as he bids them, taking the time to read the address carefully. They heatedly debate where it is and the best way to get there.

When he comes to a fork in the path and goes wrong, they languidly catch up to him and steer him right. A lesser man might be intimidated but Wormwood pays them no heed as they step in line behind him.

'Thanks, lads.'

They start to chat and he finds them good company. There is something about the sureness of his step that seems to draw them along, perhaps sensing that there is purpose to his peregrinations and that it might be worth their while to hang around, given the dearth of melodrama, teenage or otherwise, during the lockdown. They are not smoking any more but the narcotic aroma follows them, seemingly having permeated every molecule of their being.

'Where are we going?' asks the most talkative of them, the leader of sorts.

'We?' says Wormwood, looking over his shoulder at the brazen young man with a wry look. 'I'm just trying to track down a man I used to know, that's all.'

'What for?'

'If you must know,' he says, 'I've got a bone to pick with him.'

The boys all look at each. Judging by the looks on their faces, it is clearly an idiom with which they are unfamiliar. 'Is that voodoo shit?' asks another.

'Seriously?' says Wormwood, shaking his head bemusedly. He stops briefly. The disconnect in their conversation is clearly not helping his clarity of thought and he temporarily allows himself to become distracted, losing the driving imperative to keep going.

They are standing atop a bank of earth that encircles a former brick pit that has been filled in to form an ornamental lake. In the near distance, he can see the lights of a shopping centre constructed in a garish sort of neo-rococo style complete with glass and steel rotunda, so that he feels like he is both looking back into the past and forward into a hazy future simultaneously. Again, he rubs his temples. 'Do they teach you nothing at school nowadays?' They are still none the wiser. 'Having a bone to pick with someone,' he explains, 'is not some kind of *voodoo shit*. It just means someone has done me wrong and I intend to confront him about it. No big deal.'

'So, are you gonna kick someone's ass?'

'I'm going to try to teach him some sort of lesson, if that's what you mean.'

'And then you're gonna kick his ass.'

Wormwood stares hard. 'Well,' he reasons, 'only if I absolutely have to.'

That makes them all laugh, and there is some small pleasure to be had in that shared macho camaraderie. Wormwood has recovered a little and sets off again. 'What do you boys do, then?'

'Do?'

'You know, when you're not following old men around at night? Do you still go to school?'

'We used to do that,' says one of them. 'Not any more.'

'So what do you do now? That was my question.'

'We're in training,' says another. He has quickened his pace to make up for lost time, and the youths are struggling to keep up.

'What for?'

'Because we have to or they stop our money.'

Wormwood is getting exasperated. One of the youths takes the slip of paper out of his hands, stares into the distance and points to a residential area over to the right, maybe five minutes away if there is a direct path. 'No. I mean, what are you training to be?'

'I dunno,' says the leader. 'It's different for all of us, but it's a complete waste of time anyway. There are never any jobs at the end of it. It's a bad joke.'

'Aren't you a bit young to be so cynical?'

Another of the boys speaks up. They are like a collective hive mind. 'School didn't want us. College is a joke. Our parents can't afford to keep us but we can't move out because we haven't got the money to rent anywhere. There's no jobs. What the hell are we supposed to do?'

They keep going as the light fails. 'Where are your girlfriends? Surely they keep you busy? Give you a reason to be alive?'

The boys shrug. 'What girlfriends? You've got to have money to attract the girls.'

Wormwood guffaws, a raucous laugh that builds and swells from somewhere deep inside. 'That is not entirely true,' he reasons. 'But you do have to have something about you that they can believe in.'

'What the hell does that mean?'

'It means, if you don't rate yourself, why should anyone else bother with you. If you don't have money, find something you can offer them.'

'Like what?' They actually sound interested in what he has to say, like he has acquired wisdom through all his trials and suffering.

'Charm?' he suggests, though as he turns and looks at them, he is not entirely convinced. 'Charisma? Talent?' He keeps going for a while but they look none the wiser for all his efforts. 'Look, boys. I can't tell you what it is. You have to discover that for yourselves. You could form a band, write music. Become master criminals. Anything you set your mind to. You just have to believe in yourselves and see where it takes you.'

'And that worked for you, did it?' It is a good question. Wormwood has to think carefully, cautiously, before he gives a response. 'Sometimes, yes. Mostly, no. You have to have luck on your side, too.'

One of the boys walks alongside him. 'And were you lucky?'

Wormwood makes a noise that is something like a laugh though it catches in his throat. 'Not often,' he says. Then he laughs for real. 'Having said that, you should have seen my latest girlfriend. She's been stuck to me for days. I couldn't get rid of her. In fact, I just had to drag her back to her husband.'

'What was she like?'

Wormwood's eye glistens. 'Like dynamite,' he says. 'She was half my age, half my size, twice as gorgeous, if you can imagine that.'

'Dynamite,' one of the young men repeats. He likes the sound of that. 'And she was your girlfriend?'

'Not really,' says Wormwood. 'I'm too old for all of that nonsense, but believe me, she was something else.'

'Lucky you.' The youth then gives Wormwood a strange look. 'Are you that guy in the papers everyone's looking for?'

Wormwood gives him a half smile and puts his fingers to his lips. Shhhhh. They are almost there. The path widens as they get closer to civilisation.

'Things will get better, boys,' says Wormwood. He is almost there. 'That's just how life is. Sometimes it seems like everything is against you, but then things come good when you least expect it. That's the beauty of it. You've just got to do the best you can and seize your moment when it comes.'

'Do you actually believe that shit?'

'Actually,' says Wormwood, 'yes, I do.' He puts his hand in his pocket and pulls out the wad of banknotes Niamh has given him, presumably straight out of her husband's wallet. He hands the money over in thick bundles to each one. Their eyes pop like paparazzi flashbulbs.

'You sure?'

'What am I going to do with it?' He is off again, though he calls to them over his shoulder in a great booming voice. 'Have a great life, boys.' As he walks, he wonders why they are so content to be complicit in the theft of their own futures, like savages cheaply bought off with baubles while ingesting drugs which fill them with toxins, choking the life out of them. He doesn't blame them. Who could possibly stand up against the greed of corporations, great global monsters without a face to recognise or a soul to appeal to or a heart to pierce? Where are the champions who can show them how to fight? He climbs a ridge and the entire estate comes clearly into view. The moon is dangerous tonight and its cool light reveals what he must do. He crumbles the piece of paper and puts it in a pocket, letting his instincts guide him on his mission.

Suddenly, he knows the way.

Chapter 21

He bangs on the door loud enough to wake the devil. He takes three deep breaths and waits for the door to crack. He hears the fumbling of a chain and heaves his great shoulder into the door, sending it flying open so fiercely that it bounces back on itself and might have closed again but for the splintered wood and the foot he sticks in the way. At the same moment, His Lordship tumbles backwards and crashes against an ornamental table in the hallway. The house is blandly nondescript, a functional modern dwelling in a soulless estate built on reclaimed land which will one day swallow up man and house and garden and all. The circle of life.

'Who is it? What do you want?' The voice is pitifully weak, calling out in a pathetic warble to the hulking silhouette framed in the open doorway with a LED streetlamp casting a glorious aurora all around.

'Who the hell do you think it is?' roars Wormwood. 'It's your nemesis. Your day of judgement is at hand.' It is not at all clear if he is being intentionally melodramatic to scare the living Jesus out of him or if he is living this moment for real; either way, it has the desired effect on the man sprawled across his own hallway. A pool of urine spreads outwards from beneath him.

'Take what you want and leave me alone,' he whimpers.

'The only thing I want,' says Wormwood, stepping into the hallway and pushing the door to, 'is justice.' He knows exactly how melodramatic he sounds and he couldn't care less, savouring the effect upon his old nemesis.

'Oh my God,' he says, suddenly realising who his assailant is as the shadows soften and he catches clear sight of Wormwood. 'It's you.' He sounds almost disappointed.

'You must have known I would come for you.'

Lord reassembles himself to a more dignified sitting position, a little less afraid once he has recognised who it is. If he assumes that their former relationship as manager and client somehow affords him some status, he is sadly misguided. 'I assumed you were dead,' he readily admits. 'But then I saw your face in the paper and I feared the worst. I suspected you might track me down.' His voice has grown a little stronger, more sure of itself. 'What the hell do you want with me?'

'I told you that already. Consider me an avenging angel.'

'You can cut that melodramatic crap!' Lord suddenly finds a scrap of defiance, if not dignity as he lies worm-like on the ground. 'Remember, I know who you really are,' he retorts. 'I've read your file.' There is a malevolent undertone to the voice now, emboldened by the power he believes resides in the knowledge he possesses about Wormwood's past. It is a blunt instrument, to be sure, but he feels sure that his adversary will cower from the damage it can inflict upon him, like a gorgon faced with the reflection of its own ugliness.

'You know absolutely nothing about me.'

'I know your real name,' he gloats from the floor. He stands slowly, first one knee and then the other. 'Byron. Byron Hill.'

'I changed my legal name,' says Wormwood, unfazed, 'but go on.'

'I know how pathetic your life has been, one abject failure after another.' The snivelling little voice has now become a sneer. 'Marriage. Fatherhood. Career.'

'Very good.' Wormwood gives a little sarcastic clap. 'Keep going.'

Lord's voice degenerates to a taunt. 'I know you are a man considered by your peers to be without honour.' He can see before he has finished speaking that his words have hit their mark.

'Honour?' It is an animalistic roar. Wormwood takes an aggressive couple of steps forward and then manages to compose himself a little. 'How can you of all people talk to me about honour?' His hands are clenched fists he can barely control. 'You had a duty of care towards us and you just left us there to rot. Where was the honour in that?'

'It was necessary,' says Lord. 'All the experts predicted things were going to be apocalyptic. Hundreds of thousands were going to die. The NHS was going to implode. We couldn't put the living in harm's way. Hard decisions had to be made, and quickly. We were just following orders.'

Wormwood spits his words back at him. 'The fascist's prayer. *Holy father, forgive us our sins. We were just following orders.*' The blood is pounding in his temples. 'You are such a coward.'

'Now who is being the hypocrite?' Lord sneers right back at him. 'You are the one who was given a dishonourable discharge from the Armed Forces.'

'You weren't there,' says Wormwood through gritted teeth. 'You weren't there. You have no idea.'

'I know what I read in the file,' says Lord, twisting the knife. 'You were branded a coward.'

'You weren't there,' says Wormwood. 'Belfast was hell. What we were being asked to do was just plain wrong. There was a small boy, wounded, just lying there...' He can't even finish the sentence. There is another voice in his head now, one he has suppressed for years. Cracked with pain, it begs him for help. *'Please, mister, do something....'* The eyes that beseech him are even worse. Even when he shuts his eyes they burn into his soul.

Suddenly, Lord is upon him, flailing wildly, trying to inflict a meaningful blow. Something hard crashes against Wormwood's head and the shock of it rather than the pain brings him back. He clamps a hand around Lord's throat and lifts him off. He is incredulous. There is a smashed Caveo mug on the floor by his feet.

'Did you just slap me, you little bitch?' He pushes Lord away from him just far away to give him the space to land a satisfying blow to that mouth which has just spoken terrible things. The impact sends him crashing back against the wall. As he sits there, stunned, Wormwood goes into the kitchen. This is a situation that suddenly requires a cup of tea. He turns on the gas and bangs a kettle onto the hob to boil, noticing as he does so that all the mugs hanging in uniform rows on hooks are branded with the Caveo logo, every single one. Talk about a company man through and through.

Lord holds a hand to his mouth and speaks through his fingers. His eyes can't hide the pain. 'How many years did you spend behind bars like an animal?'

'You've read my file,' says Wormwood bitterly. 'I lost count.'

'And then no one wanted to touch you, you filthy disgrace of a human being.' He spits out bits of broken tooth and blood. 'And we took you in when no one wanted anything to do with you. I personally agreed to take you on, and what did we get in return?' He pauses melodramatically. 'Abuse. Attitude. Anti-social behaviour.'

'And that's just the A's,' says Wormwood wretchedly. 'And yet, as terrible as I am, you are the one who left vulnerable people to die.'

'I had a choice to make,' says Lord defiantly, 'and I chose the living over the dead.'

'But we weren't dead, you bastard. Some may have been dying, but we were still people. How could you even conceive of such a thing?'

'You think it was my idea? The shareholders demanded it. It was purely an economic decision. It wasn't easy, in some cases, but let's be pragmatic, shall we. You were as good as dead already.'

'You have no idea,' says Wormwood despairingly. 'It was pure hell. It was all we could do to let some of those poor souls die with a shred of dignity.'

'What do you want? A medal?'

'I've already been given medals,' he spits. 'I threw them all away.'

There is a brief moment of silence. Both men breathe heavily, but that is all. Suddenly, Wormwood feels exhausted. His limbs hang heavy. He can hear the whoosh of blood straining to feed his ancient body. He is aware of a sharp pain in his chest and for the first time some doubt creeps in. What does he want? Nothing can change the past, bring people back from the temporary graves in which they have been dumped with as much ceremony as he could muster.

'More than anything else,' he says falteringly, 'I want to know that you actually give a damn. I want to know that the lives of all those people actually meant something. Because otherwise, what was the point? Were all of our lives just meaningless?'

It comes to him then, all of it at once, the sense that all our lives are just an accidental exercise in biology, a fusion of cells that divide and multiply to infinity, with no greater purpose than to replicate itself, as blind and futile as the virus that has brought the world to its knees. The very idea of it overwhelms him.

The kettle whistles shrilly, bringing him back to himself again. He judges that Lord has no fight left in him and goes to pour out water into two mugs, noticing absent-mindedly how much his hand is shaking. He carries the two mugs back into the hall where Lord lies sits crookedly against a wall, a hand gingerly touching his damaged mouth. Wormwood passes a mug down to him, taking a little care not to spill any.

'You look like a two sugars kind of man to me,' he says. He leans against a wall a little unsteadily and takes a sip, savouring the sweetness, feeling the sugar revive him. 'That's better.' He stares at the Caveo logo on the mug, wonders how many meetings must have taken place to select the perfect design, precisely the right shade to convey the desired message: *We are the experts. You are safe in our hands. Pay us well.*

'It's them you really want to go after,' says Lord, desperately. He spits again, red and frothy. He whistles now when he speaks. 'I'm just a cog. Why not go after the whole machine?'

Wormwood nonchalantly takes a sip of tea but you wouldn't have to know him well to see that he is intrigued. He turns his head slowly. 'Go on,' he says.

'There have been mass protests in London at their Head Office. They have never been more vulnerable. The press have been digging up dirt. People are suddenly sick of the way they have manipulated the crisis to boost profits.' If he hopes that Wormwood has failed to notice his impersonal use of language in his implied criticism, he is very much mistaken. There is no *we* here, now that he is in pain and in fear for his safety. Suddenly, anything goes. 'If something like this went public,' he suggests, 'it could just be the spark that lights the fuse. Ordering the abandonment of a care home. You could really strike a blow against the people who screwed you over, the ones who actually made the decisions.'

'Why would you tell me this?' says Wormwood. 'It implicates you, too.'

'I was careful to leave a message trail that registered my protests,' says Lord. 'You know, just in case.'

'Even while you did exactly what you were told.'

'Exactly that. If you left my name out of it, I could tell you exactly where to go, what to do, who to point the finger at to blow this whole thing up in their faces.'

Wormwood waves his mug, corporate logo face front. 'What happened to your loyalty all of a sudden?'

Lord shrugs. 'I guess I'm feeling a little bit expendable right now,' he says. 'A bit surplus to requirements, as it were. I did my duty. Now I've been furloughed. I was hoping I meant a little bit more to them than... this.' He makes an empty gesture.

A grim laugh leaves Wormwood's throat. 'Welcome,' he says, 'to my world.' He takes another swig of tea, larger this time. He gives His Lordship a curious look. 'You really are the serpent, aren't you?'

Intuitively, he has picked up that Lord is looking not at him but beyond him. He turns, just in time, as a large figure lunges at him from behind, catching him with a substantial glancing blow that knocks him from his feet but inflicts no significant harm. With surprising agility, he is quickly back up on his feet and in a crouched defensive pose. Before he can collect his senses, huge arms grip him from behind and he feels himself constricted, lifted from his feet. He smashes his head backwards with savage force and he is instantly released. The two men exchange blows, trying to knock each other's heads off and then holding on to catch their breath. With a huge effort, Wormwood forces the younger man off him then, cautiously, backs up against a wall to survey what he is up against. The light is poor but the first man is clearly the security guard from the bank; the severe bruising to the right cheekbone and bloodshot eye testament to their previous encounter. The second man is unfamiliar but similarly formidable in size and with a considerable age advantage. Lord poses no immediate threat, but Wormwood factors him into his immediate survival strategy nonetheless. He knows he needs to be quick about his work; with each passing second, the odds grow worse.

With a feral battle-cry, he lunges at his second assailant, spinning him round to shield him from the security guard; he has already been wounded and therefore is more vulnerable to a second assault. The man is complacent, clearly underestimating the threat that an old man can pose and is content to clumsily parry the first attack, leaving his throat open to a sudden short punch that crushes his larynx with a sickening pop. Soundlessly, he slumps to his knees. A sharp kick to the head does for him. The guard instinctively takes a step back, giving Wormwood the tactical advantage. He takes two short steps forward to give his attack greater momentum. The guard is over-protective of his smashed cheek, allowing Wormwood the freedom to aim a short kick to the knee, forcing it where it does not want to go. The man is a bully not a boxer, used to overpowering smaller men with his bulk in spite of technical weaknesses to his fighting style. He goes down easily, screaming at the hot pain that shoots up through his knee to the deep core of his body. By keeping his movements as small as possible, Wormwood is able to maintain his balance, though he is breathing hard. He knows he has maybe five seconds to finish this before he runs out of air. There is a fire in his chest and waves of darkness that start to interfere with his vision, though he still has the wherewithal to make sure that Lord is suitably intimidated to remain sheepishly in the corner of the room.

The guard is open to further attack, clutching his knee with both hands, his mouth stretched open in silent agony like a scream in slow-motion. There is no place for mercy here. Wormwood puts his foot hard into the guard's damaged face and then twice more, snapping his head back until he is still.

It is done.

Wormwood takes a step back from the carnage, trying to control his breathing which is ragged and irregular. Cool moonlight slants through the windows lending an eerie calm to the room. From the corner, Lord fidgets nervously, trying to make himself as small as possible. He tries to avoid eye contact with Wormwood, who he sees now in a new light, a bestial warrior, simultaneously less than a man and much more. The violence to which he has just borne witness is not a part of the world he lives in, and he is shocked. The conflict that exists in his world is the inner battle of people at the end of their lives fighting to die well. He tries hard not to stare at the figures who lie prone across his expensive wooden flooring, blood seeping slowly into the polished grain, following grooves and channels carved by nature. If their chests are moving, he is unable to discern any sign of it, but he does everything he can not to look, scared to see in their awful stillness a forecast of his own fate. It may not have taken a genius to work out that he might be next of Wormwood's deranged list of targets, but when he arranged for protection he had never imagined that it would go down like this. Spattered with the blood of others, it is hard for him to imagine that things wouldn't have gone better if he had just faced Wormwood on his own, man to man, and tried to reason with him. Apologise, even.

'What now?' he says. His voice is like the hushed whisper of a child scared of the dark, seeing imaginary demons in the shadows, trying to be brave.

'You're read my file,' Wormwood reminds him. His voice, too, is changed a little, laboured and breathless. 'What do you think?'

Instinctively, Lord's eye flick upwards to recall details he ready long months ago. 'What do I think?' he repeats. 'A man who attacked a fellow soldier on the front line...' He is unable to complete the sentence, not caring for the line it follows.

'A man who punched a soldier who shot a young boy in the chest.'

'Shot him with a rubber bullet,' says Lord. 'A youth who was probably armed.'

'With what? A fucking rock?' says Wormwood savagely. 'A catapult?' He breathes hard. 'The kid died,' he says. 'What does it matter what I did after that.'

'How typical of you to sympathise with terrorists. You incited a mob in a war zone,' Lord reminds him. 'Soldiers' lives were put at risk by your actions.'

'He wasn't a terrorist, just a kid in the wrong place. What we did was sinful. I always believed I was a good man,' he says. His head drops. 'I was wrong.'

The adrenaline that has kept him upright suddenly dissipates and he slumps to his knees in the moonlight, like a tragic statue memorialising all the lives destroyed in that terrible moment. The family he believed he had been fighting for. The boy, whose name he can no longer suck from his ravaged memory. His own. Lord has got to his feet, sensing that the momentum in the room has shifted to his advantage. The serpent climbing the tree. With a visible effort, Wormwood turns his head, points like a preacher full of wrath.

'No, he says. 'You don't get away that easily.' He clicks his fingers and Lord freezes. 'I'm going to give you the same chance you gave us at St Peters.'

'What does that even mean?'

Wormwood goes into the kitchen. He has left the gas turned on when he made the tea, but he wrenches the pipe from the wall just to make sure. There is an instant unmistakeable odour.
'They are still alive,' he says, 'in case you were wondering. Now you have a choice. I would guess you have less than a minute before the whole place goes up. Are you going to do the decent thing and try to save them, or are you just going to slither away to save your own skin?'

'You can't do this,' Lord screams at him, eyes bulging with fear, but he is already at the front door which lolls brokenly on its damaged hinges. He searches for further insults but fear now renders him mute.

'They are bad men,' says Wormwood simply. 'They would have done worse to me. And frankly, I'm past caring.' He lights a match from a box he has found in the kitchen, drops it into the drawer with the remainder and tosses it into the house over his shoulder.

He knows the way from here even though he has only taken it once before. The further he goes, the more the evening is illuminated brilliantly by the inferno that quickly catches behind him. The roar is ferocious, like someone has pried open a route to hell. A soothing breeze has picked up which is just as well as every step he takes requires great effort. Mechanically, he puts one foot in front of the next. Even this becomes problematic. He stumbles, regains his balance, keeps going.

'Hey, mister.' Bent double, cursing for breath, he looks up and sees the youths he encountered a few hours ago. 'You okay? You don't look so good.'

He straightens up. 'I'm fine,' he says. I'm just a bit short of breath.'

The boys are sitting on a wall that is incongruous in its surroundings, as it serves no obvious function. Wormwood observes that one of them has written a slogan in huge letters so that it can be read from the nearby ring-road: **RESISTANCE IS FERTILE**.

'What's happened to your face?' One of them points at a bruise on the side on his face. A trickle of blood has seeped down under his collar.

'Oh that,' he says, wiping the blood away. 'I just fell, that's all. I'm fine.'

They don't contradict him, but they are clearly concerned. For some time, they walk along with him. His pace is considerably slower than before, and his breathing is more ragged, his speech less clear. After a short while, they reach a fork in the path. One road circles round to the far side of the estate; the other leads across fenland, and far off in distance, the sea.

'You sure you're okay?'

He nods. 'I'm good,' he says reassuringly. 'But thanks for seeing me this far.' Catching his breath has become quite a challenge and he has to make an effort to control his breathing to form the words.

'We've been talking,' says the most extrovert of the group. 'There's a demonstration tomorrow. In London. Loads of people are going from all over. It's time for a change, like you were saying. This should be our time now.'

'I'm glad,' says Wormwood, mustering a smile from deep within. 'Look after yourselves. These things have a habit of turning nasty.' They grin at each other.

'Is this what you meant?' asks the leader. 'About making our voices heard and all that.'

'Well, boys. It's a pretty good start.'

He sets off again and waves at them as he receded into the gathering shadows. They look out into the darkness in the direction of travel and watch him go with something approaching awe.

'Where exactly are you going?' one of them calls after him.

He takes a few more steps before he answers. 'Home,' he says, happily. 'I'm going home.'

They stand and watch until the darkness has swallowed him. The air is cool now, refreshing. With each step he moves on like a toy with a wind-up mechanism that is compelled to keep going, but there is another force at work, like gravity, pulling him down. His feet slip and slosh through mud though it has not rained for some days. He hears the rhythm of the blood in his veins, an unsteady whoosh that becomes voices, ancient voices both male and female, inviting, friendly, loving, urging him to stop. He has an unshakeable feeling that he has walked this land many times before through the centuries. He loses his footing, slips to his knees, panting hard though he is in no distress. Everything is calm. The urge to close his eyes overtakes him and he sinks onto his back into pacific moss, his body cruciform as if he is floating on a gentle sea. He feels the sensation of tendrils enveloping his body, easing him down through substrata of organic matter that has flourished and passed on, its energy dissipating into something old but new. He closes his eyes and his inner world is filled with a serene light which washes over him.

And after that, there is nothing.

A pair of feline eyes glisten in the darkness like precious stones. Cautiously, a solitary tiger walks up to the prone figure. It sniffs half-heartedly. It carries a small muntjac deer in its jaws, the rib-like face lolling obscenely. Lazily, it raises a leg, urinates and casually disappears into the beautiful night.

Printed in Great Britain
by Amazon